Rescue Me

Sue Bordley

ISBN: 1720557640
ISBN-13: 978-1720557647

This book is dedicated to the real-life Lauras and Jeanettes: women who help other women every day.

ACKNOWLEDGEMENTS

Huge thanks are due to my family and friends for enduring me talking endlessly about this book at every stage of its development.

Amy London from Tootle Pip Art – for making the silk purse that is this book's cover from the sow's ear that was my original sketchy design.

Thanks also to all of the staff at The Oval and Europa Pools, Wirral, but especially Jonathan the lifeguard for his help with my research.

1

The cool water laps around my ears as I lay on my back. I float, oblivious to everything and everyone around me in my own personal paradise, until...

"Oh Mummy, it's so cold, I want to get out!"

Jamie, my four-year-old daughter, starts stamping her feet and splashing at the shallow, chlorine-scented water's edge. We've got a great local pool: there's the 25-metre rectangular standard pool for the serious lane swimmers, but if you're just into playing and paddling like us, there's also a fantastic shaped pool with a sloping shallow end that you can walk straight into. I like to imagine I'm on a beach as I feel the water sloshing around my ankles, which isn't too hard because the décor's designed to have that effect, with blue mosaic tiles on the bottom of the pool, sand-yellow tiles at what would be the water's edge and even fake rocks and palm trees. Some might say it's a bit cheesy, but I think it's great.

"You'll get used to it, love, don't worry," I tell her. Sure enough, within a couple of minutes she's happily dashing towards the fountains. She loves the way the jets tickle her back. I have to admit, I sometimes sit under the fountain and have my back tickled for a few minutes as well. I miss that.

It's Tuesday morning and I don't have to go to work until this afternoon, when Jamie goes to nursery. This is my last year with her before she's in school full time, so I don't want to waste any of it. We go to the park when we can, make cakes (or at least, I make them and she throws sprinkles all over the kitchen, sometimes landing on the cakes) and today is Water Babes day. Fun and frolics for the under-fives. They play nursery rhymes over the speakers and the kids do dancing and games in the water. She loves it.

After the session, we dry off, get dressed and have our weekly treat of an early lunch in the leisure centre's café. For an establishment that's supposed to be devoted to fitness the menu's not exactly the healthiest, but as we place our regular order of chips, Diet Pepsi for me and strawberry milkshake for her, we feel we've earned it after all the jumping about.

Afterwards, I drop Jamie off at nursery, then nip back home to pop our wet swimming stuff in the wash and change for work. I work as a sales negotiator at an estate agency on my local high street, part time at the moment; maybe when Jamie's in school properly I might see if they can give me full time.

I like the job. It's interesting because no two property sales are ever the same, and of course it's fascinating to get a look round other people's houses. You do get some really obnoxious customers who seem to think it’s your fault their house isn't selling when they're the ones who picked those ugly as sin bathroom tiles, or people who turn up half an hour late for their viewing appointment and get then angry because you had the temerity to leave to be on time for your next client, but most of time, it's alright.

After work, I pick Jamie up from my in-laws and start making dinner. Chicken pasta tonight. I've been trying to get her to be a bit more adventurous with vegetables recently. Red peppers in the rice last week were a definite failure, but I do have a bit more luck with the mushrooms hidden under the grated cheese tonight.

This evening's a fairly ordinary one. Sometimes I'll take Jamie to the park to tire her out before bed, but it's a bit rainy out there tonight, so she puts on a show for me in the front room, coming out from behind the curtains and twirling about in her Disney Princess costume. I wish they'd had them when I was little. I used to have to make do with my mum's clothes when I played dress-up. Mind you, when I was a kid mums still wore dresses and skirts most of the time. Even if you couldn't get a mini version of every character from the latest film for £14 at any supermarket, I doubt Jamie would be too keen to try on my 'mum uniform' of jeans, jumpers and ballet pumps.

Once I've put her to bed, I usually just watch telly 'til it's time for me to go up as well, or sometimes, like tonight, I head up to bed myself and watch it there. Don't judge me, but I'm a sucker for reality TV. Only some of them, mind. I still think there's an interesting 'social experiment' vibe to some of the ones where they put strangers together in a house or whatever. No matter how much they all say they'll let things wash over them at the start and just get along with everyone, within a week it'll have turned into 'Lord of the Flies.' And I like the ones where you get to learn about some bizarre world you never even knew existed in the ice caps of Canada or wherever. I can't be doing with anything with the words 'Real Housewives' in the title, though. So you married a rich bloke and you can faff about all day arguing. Fine, but why should I care?

When I'm ready to drop off, I click off the telly and shut my eyes. The last thing I do every night, without fail, is whisper, "Goodnight, Shaun. Love you."

I met him ten years ago. I'd just finished uni and was working as a temp in the admin department of a small firm of solicitors until I could find something better... although even at that stage, I was losing faith in the possibility that I'd find something that'd allow me to make use of my degree, and earn the kind of money we were always told a university education would bring. As it was, I was hoping the woman I was covering for on maternity leave would decide not to come back so I might have a shot at her not-much-more-than-minimum-wage job.

It was a Wednesday lunchtime. I used to bring my own lunch to avoid buying expensive meal deals from the shop over the road, and I'd take it to the park, which was a few minutes' walk away. At first, I thought it'd be a nice way to get some peace and quiet, but really it was just full of office workers doing exactly the same as me; the common was a mass of people in rolled-up sleeves trying to get a bit of sunbathing in, or reading paperbacks.

I'd usually pass the time with a bit of people-watching. Everyone does it from time to time, don't they? Obviously, I'd do it from a reasonable distance, not sit gawping at them like a weirdo. I'd look at what people had for lunch (Ooh, I see you've gone for a flatbread, very trendy) or see if I could guess what they were reading before they lifted up their book and I could see the cover ('Based on the major motion picture!', yawn) and imagine other details in their lives: where they worked, what they did at the weekend and what their boyfriends/girlfriends/whoever would be like, or if they even had them.

I didn't imagine anyone would be doing the exact same thing about me.

"Excuse me, love, could you help me?"

I'd seen him here before. He looked about 25, and he was dressed in the trousers and shirt that marked him out as an off-duty worker like me. No tie though, I could see that lying on the grass next to his copy of 'Men's Health'. Hmm, a bit conflicting with the McDonalds I'd seen him eat last Friday. Still, a little bit of what you fancy...

And I have to admit, I did fancy him a bit. Even when he was tipping the last of his fries into his mouth, I was still thinking, I definitely would. I often gave the people I watched nicknames; that day, he became Big Mac.

"I was just wondering if you knew where that new Mexican place is, Churritos?"

Now I was actually able to look directly at him, rather than from the side as I sat on the grass with my sandwich, I could see he really wasn't bad at all. The first thing I noticed was how tall he was; even though he was sitting down, I guessed he had to be around six-two. Brown hair, cut quite short, with stunning – hazel, grey? - eyes. Either way, this was the best lunchtime in ages. The only human interaction I'd usually get would be if some idiot cyclist wasn't looking where they were going and nearly ran me over.

I did know the place he mentioned, although I hadn't been. It hadn't been open for long, but they had some Mariachi band trotting up and down the street my office was on when they opened, annoying the hell out of everyone who had to get on with their jobs, but now really fancied forgetting about work and spending the afternoon getting hammered on Tequila Slammers instead.

I pointed to the high street at the edge of the common. "Sure, it's over there, past the bank. You can't miss it." I started to put my ball of foil from my sandwich and my half-finished bottle of water into my bag when he said,

"Right, no excuses then. See you there tonight, half seven."

I dropped my bottle and laughed. "You're a cheeky bugger! What makes you think I'm interested?"

Hmm, probably my blushing cheeks and my embarrassed grin. He told me that later.

I have to admit, I definitely liked him. He was a cheeky bugger alright, but a funny one, I thought to myself. Good-looking too. Maybe not quite male model material, but who wants that really? What's the point in being with a man who's physically perfect, but spends more time in front of the mirror than you? No, I'll give you a go, I thought. You look like you could be a bit of a laugh.

I looked at him, trying not to look too excited, which wasn't easy given that my lips were once again breaking into a treacherous smile. "Okay, there's probably nothing on telly tonight anyway."

His face burst into a huge grin and he winked. I was going to see that wink a lot over the coming years.

"I knew you wouldn't be able to resist. I'm Shaun, by the way. What's your name? I can't keep calling you Tinfoil Tina, can I?"

I shook my head as I laughed again. Then I blushed. Great, I remember thinking, the one thing he's noticed about me is that I'm either skint or cheap.

"I'm Nikki," I said as I got up to leave. "I've got to go back to work now, but see you later, Big Mac."

And from then on, that was us. Tinfoil Tina and Big Mac – not that he had one of those every day, and not that we called each other those names out loud or anything, we weren't that tragic. Our lunchtimes would be spent together whenever we could synchronise them. He worked as a salesman in a mobile phone shop, and his hour out could vary depending on whether or not they had a lunchtime rush of schoolkids in. Not just lunchtimes, as going out every Friday night led to staying in bed for much of most Saturdays.

However, sad as it sounds, as time went on I'd teasingly call him Tinfoil Tom when we were saving every penny for a deposit for our first flat.

Then the wedding.

It was the perfect day. I wasn't the kind of girl who'd dreamed of a big white wedding and doodled dress designs since she was six years old. No, our wedding was a small, sweet affair: registry office then a meal (at Churritos, where else? Hey, they threw in free tequila shots when we told them) for close friends and family, far more romantic than some flashy nightmare in a castle. He got himself a new suit which he used for work afterwards, and I got a nice dress for about £50 in the Coast outlet shop. That was the way we did things. No over the top crap. For us, it was about the marriage, not the wedding.

Once we were Mrs and Mrs Dunne, the next step was getting our first home of our own.

After shooting through the roof for years, house prices actually came down the year we got married, so after about eight months of hard saving and overtime (and getting sick to the back teeth of beans on toast), were able to afford our own three-bed terrace in a fairly nice area.

With his cheeky persuasive charm, Shaun was an amazing salesman, so he was making pretty good money and I'd even got a permanent job at a different estate agency to the one I'm at now. Considering I fell into it (which everyone who does it seems to, when have you ever heard a little kid say, 'When I grow up, I want to be an estate agent,'?) I seemed to be able to hit my targets without too much difficulty. Life was good. I had a man who could make me laugh, loved me to bits and I knew we were set to have a blast together – for life.

All of that changed when I got the knock on the door.

2

I'd already noticed he was late home. At first I was a bit annoyed with him, and left his dinner to go dry and curly in the oven while I had mine in front of the soaps, not prepared to wait for him.

As I got up to answer, I thought, if he's gone for a drink with Matty again and can't be bothered rooting around for his keys, I'll kill him. Then I saw a black and white figure through the patterned glass of the front door.

I froze. Shaun should have been home two hours ago. Unless you're some kind of occupational criminal, everyone knows there's only one reason a policeman's going to knock on your door.

He was about fifty, and I could see from his

face that he knew that what he was about to say was going to destroy me. As he asked if I was the next of kin of Mr Shaun Dunne, I already had tears in my eyes and my lips were trembling. "No, no, go away!"

I tried to shut the door, as if not letting him tell me would somehow mean it hadn't happened.

The officer could see that despite what I'd said, I obviously was Shaun's wife.

Widow.

He pushed the door gently. I hadn't completely closed it. "Please, Mrs Dunne, can I come in? My name's DS Oliver. I really think it'd be best if you went inside and sat down."

I took my hand away from the door, and DS Oliver stepped inside. He gently guided me through the hallway and into my living room. Not ours any longer. Just mine.

My dinner plate was on the coffee table. I'd meant to go and wash up after the second 'Coronation Street'. The policeman found the remote and switched off the telly. While he did so, I could see him glancing at one of our wedding photos, in a frame over the fireplace. He then sat on the edge of the armchair opposite me and confirmed what I already knew.

Shaun had been driving home at his usual time, around six. It was quicker for him to do one junction of the motorway to get to our suburb, rather than weave through the rush-hour traffic of the city centre. He was always a fast driver, but he was never reckless. He was too mad about his car to ever risk losing his licence through too many speeding tickets. He had a black Nissan Pulsar GTiR, a proper Japanese import. He used to joke that the car had been with him longer than I had, and if he ever had to choose... even when we were saving up like mad for the house and wedding, his beloved Pocket Rocket was the one thing I knew not to ask him to give up. It wasn't a particularly big car and he said he was often asked why someone as tall as he was didn't go for an Impreza or an Evo, but he just loved it.

DS Oliver confirmed that it was, without doubt, the other driver's fault. They'd come up the outside lane too fast, without checking the visibility ahead, and had to slam on to avoid hitting the car in front. This meant they ended up spinning out and hitting the car in the middle lane, which in turn hit Shaun, whose car was indicating for the exit, according to witnesses. The middle lane driver sustained some injuries, but it looked like they were going to live. Not like my Shaun.

I know it sounds bad, but there and then I didn't really care about the other person. All I could think of was how I'd never see my husband again. None of this was in the plan. We were supposed to do everything together, from going on a holiday somewhere hot next year if we could save up enough, through to embarrassing the hell out of our teenage kids in the future.

When you enter into a marriage, of course you know one of you will be first to die. It's an unavoidable fact of life. It shouldn't have been like this, though. Shaun's death should have been years from now, and he should have had me, and our kids and maybe even grandchildren there with him. He shouldn't have died alone on a motorway just because of some idiot's impatience.

Nearly six years later, I still can't really remember everything about the weeks immediately after his death. There was his funeral, of course. In a church, the one he'd been baptised in twenty-nine years earlier. He'd long since stopped believing, which is why we never got married there, but I agreed when his parents said it was what they wanted. I could see they needed to feel things had been done properly. Yes, I was his wife, but they were a mum and dad doing the last thing they could for their son. It had to be their way.

I just about held it together during the service. I needn't have really concerned myself with that though; everyone around me was being really supportive and no-one would have been surprised or thought any less of me if I'd have gone to pieces. The only time I cried was as his coffin was led out of the church, to a song that I didn't listen to much before and have had to switch the radio station if it were to come on since: Green Day's 'Good Riddance.' He used to say it the only one by them he liked, and even suggested we have it as our wedding dance (before we realised we didn't need a wedding dance at all and jibbed the idea), because he hoped it'd be the time of our lives. Anyone who knows the song will tell you that's kind of missing the point, but there was no other song I could consider to say goodbye to him.

After the funeral, it was time to get on with life without him. Sure, his friends and mine all promised they'd make sure I was okay, and his parents assured me I was still their daughter-in-law and that we should stay in touch, but what was the point of life now? Everything I'd planned, everything I'd expected to happen had been taken away. I'd picked the wrong box in the gameshow of life, and now I had to leave with nothing.

My doctor gave me a note for a couple of weeks off, but after a while I thought it might be better if I went back to work. Everyone had been very kind, sending me a bouquet and a card. A couple of colleagues were allowed the morning off to attend the funeral. I was just about managing, probably helped by the fact that the branch manager shifted me towards working on commercial properties for a while. He didn't give me a reason for it, but I imagine he thought it wouldn’t be great for me to be exposed to jolly first-time buyer couples looking for their dream homes every weekend. Whether it was just so I wouldn't make the company look bad when I started howling during a viewing, or because he was genuinely concerned for me, either way I was grateful.

Then, about six weeks after Shaun's death, the sickness began. Even though I'd never experienced morning sickness before, and at first it hit me in the evenings, after a few days I had no doubt that was what it was. That, combined with the missed period I hadn't even noticed while we were all caught up in the funeral arrangements. Given my circumstances, when I told my GP they rushed me through for a dating scan and they were able to confirm I was almost eight weeks pregnant.

I couldn't believe it. We knew we definitely

wanted to have kids some day and even talked a bit about actually trying for one, but we weren't sure it was the right time yet. We were still young, he said, we had years left to have kids. But now, at 27, I wasn't just a grieving widow. Now I was a woman facing the prospect of bringing up a child alone.

"You're not doing this alone, we're here for you. Remember that." As you can imagine, Shaun's parents were delighted when I told them. Well, maybe that's not the word, but you know what I mean.

"This child will be surrounded by a family that loves it, we'll make sure it has everything it needs," Alan, his dad, said. "Everything."

Tears trickled down Christine's face. A common thing since Shaun's death, but this time she was smiling as well. "It's a miracle," she said, wiping her eyes. "We've still got something of him. He's not completely gone."

I wasn't surprised by their reaction. Of course they'd feel some reassurance, some hope, from knowing that although they'd lost their son, they would still get to see his child. It'd give them some comfort to think he'd be living on through this baby.

I understood all of that, but the only emotion I remember experiencing was fear. There was no way I could, or wanted to even consider not keeping it, but would I be able to cope? How could I look at Shaun's baby every single day without it feeling like a knife to the heart? I was hardly managing to look after myself since he'd gone, how on earth was I ever going to be able to look after another human being?

I had no choice but to find out.

Seven months later, Jamie was born. I know people might have expected me to call her Sian or Shauna, but I couldn't face the thought of giving this tiny newborn, with her whole life ahead of her, her dead father's name. His middle name was James, so Jamie it was.

Both Christine and my mother were in the room. You're only supposed to have one person with you, but seeing as that person's usually the father, I think they made an exception.

I imagine all women cry the first time their baby is held to their chest to get the smell of its mother and make the bond with her, but my tears weren't just relief that she'd been born safely. Throughout my pregnancy, I'd had to do a lot of things alone (I know his parents said they'd be there for me, but I couldn't exactly ask them to do things like cut my toenails towards the end when I found it hard to reach, or to give me a backrub, which some of the women at work had told me had been really helpful for them) but meeting our child was the hardest thing I'd had to do without Shaun yet. In fact, ever.

And that was that. I was a mother. Jamie and I have muddled along well enough for the last four years. She's an angel, the apple of all of her grandparents' eyes. All the doubts I had were completely unfounded. Having her to care for gave me something to focus upon, a reason to keep going when otherwise I might have given up. She is my miracle and I couldn’t imagine life without her.

Well-meaning work colleagues said things along the lines of maybe it was for the best that Shaun didn’t know about her. Not to my face, of course. I heard Jen say it to Karen once while they were washing their hands, not realising I was in the end cubicle. I know what they mean by that: he'd have loved to have been a dad, and he'd have been brilliant. Then she'd said how horrible it would have been for him to die, knowing that his last thoughts would have been that he wouldn’t get to see his child.

He does know, though, and he can see her. Like I said, we weren't religious, but I believe he's there when I say goodnight to him. I know he can see Jamie, and I know he loves her as much as I do.

3

"Thanks for coming in, Nikki," Jeanette, my boss, says. "I know this is your morning off, but I couldn't really fit this in at any other time."

"No problem," I reply, although if I'm honest, it is a bit awkward. Jamie only does afternoons at nursery, and forget about the idea of grandparents being 24/7 babysitters. All of her grandparents still work. Not many people in their sixties are retired anymore. In the end, I had to beg a favour from a mate and ask her to have her for a while.

"Okay, I'll make this as quick as I can," she begins. "This branch of Crostons is opening a Lettings department. Think about it. Almost every terraced house we sell is to a developer who then wants to rent it out. Some of them are even cheeky enough to ask if we can give them a list of our first time buyers. There's a huge market out there, and we're not just going to get a piece of it. We're going to dominate it."

I try to keep a straight face. I love Jeanette, really, but she can be a bit full-on with the motivational office-speak sometimes. You can always tell when Head Office have sent her on a course, she'll have a new catchphrase for a week afterwards.

Lettings department? Great, I think. Sounds like a smart idea. In fact, something I think I said to her a while ago, when one of my cousins was looking for a place and thought I'd be able to help him, but I couldn't because I only dealt with sales.

"Now, I know this is something you've shown some interest in before, Nikki, so I'm going to give you the chance to head up the Lettings department. If you're interested."

"I'm definitely interested, Jeanette," I tell her.

This is brilliant. More responsibility, the chance to run a department of my own... and she hasn't said so yet, but it's got to mean a pay rise as well, hasn't it?

"There is one thing though," she says. "If you're going to take this position, we're going to need you to work full-time. Five days, including some weekends."

I take a sip of my drink, not because I really want one, more to give myself a chance to think of what to say next. Okay, the weekend thing is no problem. I do a couple of Saturdays a month now on a rota with the other staff while Jamie has a day of getting spoilt rotten by either one of her nans. And I did want to ask about going full-time when she starts school in September.

Trouble is, it's June now. It'd probably be pushing it to ask Jeanette if she'd be willing to wait 'til then, but how annoyed would I be, having to watch someone else doing the job I could have had? Then there's the money. I'd be missing out on an extra two days' wages, and whatever I might get from the promotion. We're not exactly on the breadline, the mortgage we'd had was paid off by the insurance when Shaun died, but that extra money would make a big difference.

I'm going to do this. No idea how, but it's on.

"I'd love to. I was hoping to move to full-time anyway, so this is a brilliant opportunity. Thanks, Jeanette. I won't let you down."

She removes her glasses, folding them before putting them down on her desk, and gives me a wry smile. "I know you won't, that's why I asked you. Tell you what, I'll let Head Office know I've found my Lettings manager, and we can meet again next week to discuss the way forward."

I arrive at Laura's place about twenty minutes later, armed with a bottle of wine as a 'thank-you' for minding Jamie. I wouldn't normally ask her to mind her at her home, because she's one of those happily childless people who lives in a spotless flat, but like I said, I was desperate and anyway, she's as good as an auntie to Jamie.

When she answers the door, she's wearing makeup... in fact, it looks like she's wearing all the makeup she owns in one go. I'm guessing she's let Jamie loose on her makeup bag. Oh hell. I know I don't really care and can make do with any old cheap brand, so I don't mind too much if Jamie has a play with my lippy and blunts it, but Laura's really into her makeup. Since being let go from her last job two months ago, she's been trying to get into doing it professionally, always asking me to share pictures of people she's done on Facebook. I don't think she's ever bought a single cosmetic item from Asda in her life, except maybe sponges, and I'm pretty sure the only three little words that she really wants to hear are 'Clinique Bonus Time.'

I immediately start totting up how much I might have to give her to reimburse her for all the Chubby Sticks Jamie's bound to have destroyed while giving Laura a makeover (and then probably using the same crayon to draw a picture or something, yikes!), but as we head through to the kitchen and she puts the kettle on, Laura tells me it's her 'Auntie Laura' bag.

"D'you think I'm soft, Nik? I'm sorry, you know I love Jamie, but there's no way she's going near my good stuff. I bought this bagful from the poundshop. I take it with me so when I'm doing someone's face, if they've got a kid with them, they can mess about with this. Occupies the kid and stops my stuff being ruined. She's been a little star. We've had a good time, haven't we, Jaybabes?"

Jamie's come running up to me by this point, with a much better makeup job, obviously done by Laura. She's even got a couple of little hearts and stars doodled around her cheekbones. Laura gives her one of the juiceboxes and a bag of rice cakes I left her with earlier and she makes tea for me, coffee for her.

I tell Laura about the outcome of the meeting, and how the only real obstacle is finding childcare so that I can manage full time. I know I really shouldn't ask her. I mean, I know she said she's enjoyed having Jamie round today, but that's probably only because of the novelty value. And anyway, how would I feel about being asked to give up my time on a regular basis?

"There's got to be a way round it, Nik. You need this."

"No need to tell me," I reply. "I just wish it had come up in September. With Jamie at school it'd be a lot easier."

Oh, what the hell.

I pause for a minute before asking. "Laura, you couldn’t do some of it for me, please? It's really only 'til when the schools finish, when you think about it."

My mum's a teacher, and while they certainly don't get the twelve weeks off or whatever it is that idiots who know nothing about their job say they get, since the arrival of Jamie, Mum's always refused to do Summer school or exam marking so she can help me out.

Laura sighs. I can see she feels a bit obligated. I feel rotten, but what can I do?

"Okay, Nik, if you put it like that. I know this is a big deal for you."

I put my cup down and give her a hug. "Thanks Laura, this'll make things so much easier. Look, it'll only be mornings, I'll pay you the proper rate and if it’s easier, have her at my house. That way, any mess she makes is my problem."

"You can't afford the proper rate," Laura says. "I don’t even know what it is, but even if it's minimum wage, you'll have no money left. Look, you can pay me in bottles of wine, or when you've got loads of fit single men looking for flats to rent, don’t find them one, just send them round here," she laughs, before adopting a comically vampy voice. "Tell them I'm fully furnished with additional extras, available immediately and offer flexible terms!"

I have to laugh. Laura's not the sort of person I would ever have thought I'd be friends with. I'm really ordinary, not much of a risk-taker, but she's the total opposite. She's out of work now because she got sacked from her last job in a care home for telling the residents too many dirty jokes. She argued they were old, not stupid and maybe they'd enjoy a good laugh. I don’t think I've ever met anyone with such a wicked sense of humour and knack for turning anything into an innuendo.

Well, maybe one person.

Anyway, it's time for me to give Jamie some lunch and take her to nursery. I say goodbye to Laura, thank her again and head for home.

After I've seen Jamie off to nursery that afternoon, I'm back at work. I'll still be working on residential sales until Head Office approve me (although Jeanette says that'll be no problem) so this afternoon, I'm doing accompanied viewings. While I'm driving out to meet an elderly gentleman and his son to show them a bungalow, I find myself thinking about what Laura said.

Fit single men looking for flats to rent. Not really, I think. More likely to be sad divorced men, looking for a miserable bedsit to bring their kids to after the obligatory trip to McDonalds every Saturday. Still, if Mr Wonderful does happen to come in, I'll certainly send him her way. I definitely owe her one.

No, I wouldn’t be interested. Men don't really figure much in my thoughts. Firstly, there's the obvious reason that Jamie's my priority. Even if I was able to attract them, it wouldn’t be right to expose her to a string of men trooping through the house. Not having ever had her father in her life, there's no need to go looking for a replacement for something she's never known. I'm all she needs, and as far the 'important male figure' that psychologists always talk about, well, Shaun's brother and her grandad love her to bits.

Then there's the other thing, less obvious but just as important. What's the point of looking for another man? I had the best there was, and he's gone. No-one else would ever be able to measure up.

I'm not totally dead inside. Of course I fancy actors or celebrities, but there hasn't been anyone in the real world since Shaun. I don't like being alone, but what's the point in being with someone, anyone, when I know all I'd be doing is thinking about the man I still love?

In the months after Shaun's death, my doctor put me in touch with a group called Young and Widowed - guess what that was about? It was run by some very kind, well-intentioned people, but to be honest, I'm not sure how it was supposed to help, exactly. When all I could think of was how hard I was finding life without the man I thought I'd be with forever, I can't say it made me feel any better to speak to other people, some who'd been coming to the group for years. I'd just leave each meeting weighed down with sadness for the other men and women who'd lost their partners, as well as myself.

Then there was the other thing. The organisers of Young and Widowed stressed that they actively discouraged people forming couples, but it still happened anyway. I guess it helped some people to find a new partner who understood what they'd been through. I had a few men from the group show a bit of interest in me, but it just didn't feel right to me. It was too soon after Shaun's death, and I got the feeling these men just seemed to be looking for replacements for the wives they'd lost. One even said I reminded him of her.

I stopped going to the group after about a year. I thought being in a room with a load of people, all of us linked by this one common characteristic none of us wanted, just wasn't healthy. I didn't want to forget or replace Shaun, but I couldn't just spend the rest of my life dwelling on the fact I was his widow either.

So I just got on with my life. Worked hard at my job, spent quality time with my girl. I guess I've just become kind of asexual. As far as I was concerned, that part of my life was over. And I can't see much happening to make that change.

4

This isn't exactly what I had in mind. I thought being the Lettings Manager would mean I'd be coming to work in a suit every day, having an office of my own and maybe even a member of staff below me. Don't get me wrong, I'm not some megalomaniac who dreams of bossing people around, I just thought being a manager would involve having someone to manage.

That's coming later, Jeanette's assured me. Once the Lettings department's up and running, she's said I can have someone to work with me. But for now, I'm on my own. While my colleagues in Sales are sat at their desks, doing the job I used to do, I'm standing by the front door of the showroom wearing a bright yellow T-shirt emblazoned with the words, "I want to see your bedroom!" on the front, and "Rent Girl!" on the back. I feel like a complete lemon, both professionally and literally.

Needless to say, I wasn't keen on wearing it. I'd turned up in a suit for today's big launch. In fact, when Jeanette showed me the T-shirt, I thought it was a joke. Oh no.

"Look, Nikki, I can see you don't like it, but there's a lot of competition out there. We've got to make ourselves memorable."

Hmm, I thought, why are you saying 'We?' As far as I can see, there's definitely only one of us who looks like a slutty banana... still, I bit my lip and reminded myself that while looking a complete div was only for one day, the £5000 pay rise would last a lot longer.

So for now, I'm trying to get the attention of people as they walk in (not hard, I guess Jeanette has got a point) and try to get them interested in either renting off their empty property, or getting their names on a list of potential tenants for when we've got said empty properties. Even that's not proving too difficult: I'll never be a political expert, but one thing I've learned about the world since I started this job is that anyone wealthy enough to have an empty property is always keen on making a few bob more, and thousands of young people are going to be geriatric before they can even get one foot on the property ladder.

By the end of the day, I think I've done quite well. Five viewings booked for prospective rental properties, and at least twenty people have expressed interest in me finding them a property to rent. Jeanette's certainly happy. So am I.

I'm absolutely shattered after such a busy day, so when I pick Jamie up from Alan and Christine, all I'm ready for is zapping something quick for tea and a glass of wine after she's gone to bed – and bedtime will definitely be a bit earlier than usual.

However, my mum's there as well. That's not hugely surprising since she and Christine actually get on quite well. They have each other on Facebook, and they even go shopping or to the theatre together sometimes. She usually says if they've got a night out planned, though.

"Right, come on, we're all going out for a meal to celebrate your first day in management! We're not taking 'No' for an answer, are we, Jamie love? You're super-proud of Mummy, aren't you?" Christine chirps

"Yeah!" Jamie says, giving me a big hug around my thighs.

I open my mouth to say that having a desk ten feet away from the one I used to have and looking like Big Bird's crack-whore cousin all day doesn't exactly constitute being management, but the thought of sitting in a chain pub (when you've got a four-year-old, you don't eat out anywhere that doesn't have a playground), having a meal just appear and getting started on that glass of wine early while Christine and Mum run around after Jamie in their latest bout of competitive nannying does sound quite appealing.

Two hours later, I'm feeling considerably better after a large drink and piri-piri chicken with sweet potato fries (I'll get salad with it next time, we all decided calories officially don't count today). Jamie's had a run around the play area, before coming back to our table when the waiter brings her Princess sundae. Between mouthfuls of ice cream and a bizarre wafer with edible glitter on it, she has a question.

"Mummy, why haven't I got a daddy?"

Oh no. I'm not ready for this.

I knew I'd have to tackle it one day, but I wanted the time to be right. I wanted to have planned what I'd tell her and know it'd make her understand and feel reassured. Most of all, I wanted it to be a discussion I initiated in which I knew what the hell I was going to say, not when I'm all full of a stodgy two-for-one meal deal and the wine I'm already regretting.

But that's the thing about being a parent. It's not about me, is it?

After a deep breath and another sip of my wine, I go for it. "Love, lots of children don't have their daddies. Ava-Grace doesn't live with her daddy, does she?" I say, hoping that might delay her until I'm feeling ready to talk about this – when she's about twenty-five, maybe. Who am I kidding? Jamie may be innocent about some of the realities of life, but she's mine and Shaun's girl: sharp as a tack and able to smell bullshit from a mile away. I found that out as soon as she could speak and I didn't have a hope in hell of getting her to fall for any of that 'Mmm, this broccoli is delicious' malarkey.

"She has got a daddy though, she just doesn't live with him. Her mummy told her they're not friends anymore so they can't live together, but she goes to his new house every Saturday. I've never had a daddy. Why not?"

I look across at her grandparents. I can see

they're as anxious as I am, but none of them say anything. I guess they think this is something that has to come from me, or they're worried about telling her in a way I wouldn't like, but as I said, I really hadn't thought this one through properly yet. I'd actually love someone to jump in and sort this out for me right now.

But that's another thing about being a parent, especially a single one. Everything's your job.

"Well, you know how you've got Nanny and Grandad Dunne, but there's just Nanna Cartwright? Well, you had a Grandad Cartwright, but you've never seen him because he's in Heaven. He went there because he was an old man, he'd had a long life. We were very sad when he went, but we know he's happy."

This does seem to have worked as a distraction. I lost my dad about ten years ago. All Jamie's ever seen of him is a picture on Mum's sideboard, and she's never really questioned why he isn't there. I know it sounds harsh, but I can handle talking about his absence a lot more easily than I can Shaun's: Dad was a good few years older than Mum, forty-eight when I was born, so from my teenage years, I understood I wasn't going to have him around all my adult life. Obviously, I expected to have longer with my husband.

"Is my daddy in Heaven as well then? Was he an old man too?"

At this point, Mum can see she needs to give me a bit of a hand. She takes Jamie and sits her on her knee.

"The thing is, love, sometimes people have to go to Heaven even if they're not old. It might be that they're sick or they get hurt, because in Heaven they get better."

I can see Jamie's brow furrow as she tries to process this. It doesn't take her long: everything's simple when you're nearly five.

"Okay. Can we go and see him next weekend then? He must be better by now," she says, hopefully.

Alan tries to make it a bit clearer. I reach for another sip of my drink. I know I didn't want to deal with this tonight, but in some ways it's been better. At least I've had other people around to help when I've obviously messed it up.

"Sorry, Jamie. People can't come back from Heaven. Your daddy can't come back, and you can't go to see him."

Jamie's smile disintegrates. "Was I a baby

when he went to Heaven?"

Oh God, what's the answer to that? If I wasn't prepared for her first question, I'm certainly not going into the birds and the bees in a Hungry Horse pub on a Saturday teatime.

Luckily, Alan smooths it over by telling her, "Yes, love, you were very, very tiny." He touches her cheek gently. "Hey, before he went, he told me to tell you that he loves you more than all the stars in the sky, though."

Of course, Alan, Christine and Mum all know that's not true, but there's no way I want this already grim conversation to go much further. Right now, I can live with Alan's white lie if it puts an end to any more questions.

Anyway, maybe it's not a complete lie. Like I said before, I know he can see her. She's no different to her friends. She has got a daddy... just not here.

Never mind true love, world peace or the meaning of life. The hardest thing in the world to find is your daughter's glasses when you have to be out of the house in five minutes. Laura decided come here to mind Jamie now

I'm working full-time, but I still have to make sure she's dressed, fed and ready. I can't take the piss and expect her to be a full-on nanny when she won't even take babysitter money from me.

"Oh hell," I mutter as I hear the doorbell, then a little more breezily, "Here's Auntie Laura! Mummy's off to work now, give me a big hug!"

Jamie runs towards me and I scoop her up into my arms, then put her down and answer the door. Right, one more minute to look for those glasses and then I'll just have to go, no matter what.

Laura walks in. "Hi, Nik. Where's my Jaybabes?" She says, as Jamie runs towards her, holding up Big Ted... who's wearing her glasses and the amber beads I got for Christmas. Great. At least I can go off to work without the guilt of thinking I'm leaving my daughter in a blurry world, or expecting Laura to find them. I remove the specs from the teddy and bend down to put them on her.

"Right, my little monkey. You be good for Auntie Laura. I want to hear you've eaten up all your lunch and I'll see you tonight. Okay?" I then look up and tell Laura, "Okay, you know where everything is, there's some money on the table to pay the window cleaner. See you later. Cheers, Laura."

And then it's off to another day at work. The Lettings department's been up and running for about a month now, and we haven't quite achieved the domination Jeanette spoke of when she first put the idea to me, but give me time... we've got a decent enough portfolio of properties, and it's going to get better, even if I have to wear that bloody T-shirt again to get people's attention.

I've even got an assistant! Well, kind of. Karen's daughter has just finished her GCSEs and, after a couple of weeks of sleeping in and recovering, was tempted by the idea of coming into work with her mum for some work experience - and a bit of money. She's not officially employed by Crostons, I think Jeanette's finding some way of bending the expenses so she can pay her something for making the tea and photocopying. Anyway, while Chelsea's here for the whole office, I'm allowed to ask her to do some tasks for me, which is making things a bit easier.

It's about half past ten. I'm sitting at my desk and Chelsea's just come in with a cup of tea for me and the pile of blank Assured Shorthold Tenancy contracts I asked her to run off. I continue compiling a set of details on a property I measured up yesterday. Bit of a waste of time, if I'm honest with myself. I mean, it's standard procedure to make up a leaflet to give to prospective tenants, it's one of the things the landlord's paying for, but I know I've already got about six people who'd be interested in renting this one-bed flat in the city centre. I'll have contracts signed on this one before Chelsea's even taken my details to the photocopier.

My daydreams about landing another contract are interrupted by a deep voice. "Erm, hello, is this the rent section?"

I turn and look up from my screen. Then up a little bit more. Wow, this guy's tall. Over six feet, easily. I stand up so I can look him in the bellybutton. Oh okay, that's an exaggeration, but I still feel pretty small next to him.

Actually, for the first time since... well, you know, I think I'm feeling something else as well. Maybe I've just got a bit of a thing for tall men, but he's quite nice. He's wearing trainers, jeans, T-shirt and a denim jacket, which looks like he's had it quite a while. Chilled but not scruffy.

"Yes, this is Lettings. How can I help you?" I can usually make a fair guess at whether people who approach my desk are potential landlords or tenants: things like their age (middle–aged people often rent off the homes they've inherited from their parents, while anyone under twenty-five is usually looking to rent a flat) and whether their clothing looks expensive, although I can get it wrong sometimes. There's a man who comes into our office regularly who looks like a scarecrow on crack, but he owns several houses in the posh end of town, so you never know.

I can't quite tell with this man, either. He looks like he's late twenties, and while his clothes are casual, how do I know whether these are his work clothes, or it's his day off? There's one thing I am sure of though: he's got stunning eyes. Dark brown, matching his hair exactly.

This feels wrong. Like I said, I've allowed myself to fancy men on the telly (I like that one who presents the local evening news at the moment), but since Shaun, I've never even given a thought to anyone in the real world. Forget about it, Nik. Come on, get your head back in the game and just do your job.

"I'm looking for somewhere to rent. I'm not too fussy about the area, well to be honest I can't be," he says, grimacing. "I'm not exactly loaded, so the cheaper the better really."

"No problem, Sir," I say, logging myself back

into my computer. "How about I take your details and then I can see what we've got that might suit you...."

After he's gone, I take a sip of my now-cold tea and a deep breath.

What the hell just happened there? According to Chelsea (and Karen and Jen, they were all gawping at me) I was grinning like an idiot and gabbling like a schoolgirl who's come face to face with One Direction the whole time I was dealing with Rob Jones. Was it that obvious I fancied him? Guess it must have been.

They teased me about it for the next hour until I went out to do a viewing. While I was driving to it, I thought about what had happened. The first time I've shown any interest in a man in over five years. What does it mean? I'm certainly not forgetting about Shaun, I'll never do that.

And anyway, this Rob's a customer. It'd be totally unprofessional to go out with him, or even fancy him. I just need to get this out of my mind and carry on... but that doesn't mean I couldn't find a way to pair him up with Laura. I know she wasn't strictly serious when she asked me to send any fit men her way, but Rob... okay, I admit it, he's pretty fit, and I definitely owe her a huge favour in return for all the free childcare.

Now I just need to think of a way to get them together.

5

"Hello, Mr Jones? Nikki Dunne from Crostons Lettings here. I was wondering what you thought of the apartment you viewed at the weekend."

It's Monday morning, and I'm doing my 48-hour follow up calls on the viewings I did on Saturday. Sometimes I don't have to do them because the tenant decides on the spot that they'll take it, but after looking round a one-bedroomed flat above a shop just outside the city centre, Rob told me he'd have to think about it.

"Oh, hi Nikki," he says. "Can you just give me a minute and I'll be with you?" As I wait, I can hear the sound of a kettle boiling on his end of the line, followed by him pouring some water into a cup.

Wonder if he's a tea or coffee person? I'm a definite tea drinker, or at least I've become one. I used to love coffee, so strong Shaun always said he wouldn't pour me a coffee, he'd cut me a slice... but I gave it up when a bereavement counsellor said they couldn't treat me if I didn't cut caffeine out of my life. Admittedly, I rarely went an hour at work without a coffee, but I was never sure why she wanted me to do that. But I did, and that was when I encountered the horror that is decaf. Seriously, what is the deal with that stuff? Looks okay, smells okay, but then you taste it... I gave Laura one once and her immediate reaction was, to use her unique turn of phrase, that it was 'like shagging a man with no dick.'

So I made the switch to tea when I'm at home or work. These days I just allow myself the odd cappuccino when I'm out, which I reckon shouldn't count 'cause they're half milk anyway.

I bet Rob's not decaf, I think to myself.

I never did do anything about trying to fix him up with Laura. I mean, how could I have gone about it? If we were in a club or bar it'd be easier, but while he's my client it's a lot more difficult. What do I do? Just accidentally-on-purpose have her turn up while I'm showing him a flat?

Anyway, Laura wasn't exactly convinced when I told her about him.

"So this six foot two, dark haired, fit tenant is a great match for *me*, eh Nik?" she teased, when she came round for a drink on Saturday night. "You know I like fair-haired blokes." Her eyes narrowed and her lips curled lustily. "Ooh, if you ever get that Freddie Flintoff in, wouldn't mind a bit of LBW with him. He could have a full toss in the crease anytime."

I have no idea what either of those two things are, just that they're things that happen in cricket, but only she could make them sound like something rude.

As I got up to fetch another glass of wine from the kitchen, I said, "Well, you said send you any fit blokes who come in..."

I came back to the living room with our drinks and sat back down.

"...and I'd say Rob is. To tell you the truth Laura," I remember taking a deep breath before continuing, "I quite like him myself."

Laura left the tortilla chip she was about to

put in her mouth hanging.

"No way," she said sarcastically. "I'd never have guessed. The way you haven't shut up about him and you go pink every time you talk about him, I thought you hated him." Then she sat up a bit straighter and picked up her glass. "Look Nik, if you like him, why don't you go after him? You can send me the next fittie who comes in."

I didn't reply. As I said, I've allowed myself to have the odd crush on people from the telly, but that's probably because I'll never meet them: when a crush lives in your head, you're completely safe from being rejected. This is the first time I've actually expressed some interest in a real person, one who might actually return my interest... or not.

She could see from my face that I was trying to find some argument against it, when really, there'd only be one reason for my reluctance.

"Nik. It's been nearly six years since Shaun..." she trailed off, not finishing the sentence.

I come across that a lot, and I admit I've been guilty of it myself from time to time. People seem afraid of the word 'death', which is stupid because it's the only thing that, no matter who you are, everyone's got in common. I've overheard people at work say, 'It must be hard for her since she *lost* her husband', as if a good tidy-up and a look down the back of the couch would bring him back.

"I know exactly when my husband *died*, thanks Laura," I snapped.

A second later I said, "Sorry, I know you're only trying to help. Trust me, I know what you're going to say: Shaun wouldn't want me to be unhappy and lonely, it's time I moved on and all those other cliches I've had people spout at me since he's been gone."

She sat next to me and put a friendly arm round my shoulder.

"They may be cliches, but there's some truth in them as well, Nik. Of course you'd still be with Shaun if he was alive, you wouldn't have looked at anyone else. But the fact is, he's not here and you're only 32. You don't deserve to spend the rest of your life alone. I didn't know Shaun that well, but I can't believe he'd want you to be lonely and miserable."

"I'm not miserable," I replied. "I've got a good job, I'm doing alright. I'm not lonely, either. I've got friends, and Jamie. That's all I need."

Despite saying that, talking about Shaun and even the prospect of being with someone else, leaving him behind, made my eyes well up. Tears forced their way out of the side of my eyes and rolled down my cheeks.

"Is it really?" Laura asked sympathetically. "Look Nik, I don't want to be a bitch and upset you any more, but..."

She paused, aware that what she was about to say might not go down too well with me.

"Yes, of course I'm here for you, and Jamie's a little angel, but there's more to life than that, isn't there? When you go to bed at night..."

I got defensive again. "We're not all obsessed with sex like you," I said, standing up and moving away from her. "I've got Jamie to think about."

Laura took a step towards me and put her hands on my forearms. "Nik, listen to me. I mean, really listen. Of course Jamie always comes first, of course you'll always love Shaun, but it's not a crime to want some happiness for yourself – and yeah, I do mean sex... among other things. Sex, fun, love – all the things you get in a relationship. You deserve that as much as anyone else, maybe more. You've had the love of your life taken away, but it doesn't mean you can't build a new life, or find a new love."

I'd dissolved into a crying mess by that point. She sat me back down and handed me my wine and a tissue.

"Sorry I called you sex-obsessed," I said, wiping my face.

"Nik, forget it," she replied. "Look, maybe we should call it a night after this glass. But if you like this Rob bloke, there's nothing wrong with seeing if it could go anywhere."

"Okay, with you now, Nikki," Rob says. "Just making myself a coffee. I'm useless 'til I've had my caffeine fix."

"Ha! I knew you wouldn't be decaf," I say triumphantly, before realising I've actually said that out loud. Damn! How do I explain this?

"Oh, I'm sorry, Mr Jones. Just wondering what drink I could offer you when you come in to sign the contracts – that's if you liked the flat, of course?"

After a pause at the other end, he says. "Err, okay. Well, I am interested, but I'm not 100% sure. Could I have another look round and bring a tape measure, so I could be sure I'd get all my stuff in?"

"No problem," I say, clicking on the appointments spreadsheet. He asks if he could view it today, but it's all booked up. Still, I'm going to make this happen.

I was angry with her at first, but Laura's right. I know I was planning to match Rob off with her, but she's made it clear she thinks he's more my type. Maybe it is time I thought about my own happiness as well as Jamie's... and I know seeing him again would definitely put a smile on my face.

"How about six o'clock? Could you make that, Mr Jones?" That's outside of the hours I usually do viewings, but he doesn't have to know that. I'll just take the keys, do it on my way home and return the keys tomorrow. If it gets another flat let out, I can't see Jeanette having a problem with it.

"Six sounds great," he says, "and please, it's Rob. Mr Jones makes me sound old."

At five to six, I'm waiting in my car outside the shop the flat's above. I check my reflection in the pull-down mirror. I look okay, but not great. I'm in my work clothes, which is what he'd expect; if I went home and changed he'd really think something was up. I've got to remember he's a client and I can't be unprofessional, not if I want to keep my job.

One last slick of lippy and I can't really do much more. I know I'm a bit excited and treating this a bit like a date, but it's just viewing a flat to him. The only kind of offer I'm going to get tonight will be if he wants to sign up.

I see him walking towards the door that leads off the road and to the flat. Just before I get out of the car, I give myself a final check in the mirror... then take off my wedding ring. My hand feels naked without it, but if I'm going to make my first attempt at moving on, I guess it's going to have to go.

"Hi... Rob. Glad you could make it. Right, let's go and have another look around."

He looks at his watch.

"Could we just wait a minute, Nikki? I want someone else to see the flat as well. Oh, it's alright, here she is," he says, as a black Mercedes parks across the road and a red-haired, pretty woman gets out. I'd guess she's about four or five months pregnant. Far along enough that you wouldn't just think she's overweight, anyway. A quick look at her left hand just puts the lid on it.

Oh. Right, let's just do the viewing then. Sorry Shaun, I think to myself, it wasn't worth taking my ring off for this.

The woman says hello to Rob and me, before asking, "Do you think this is it then, Rob?"

"Yeah. I've looked at a few flats, but this is the only one I've come back to. Maybe this'll be the one," he says, following me up the stairs.

Well, that's what I thought. Oh well, maybe I can at least get some commission out of this. I open the front door which, because the flat is above a shop, leads immediately to a staircase. Rob gestures for me to go first, then tells the other woman to hold on to the handrail because the stairs are a bit steep, saying, "You've got to be careful." I feel a pang of jealousy; no husband there to be concerned about me when I was pregnant.

As he's seen the flat before, I don't tell Rob where anything is. Instead, I show the woman round. I know it's not really any of my business, but it's a one-bedroom flat and they'll clearly be needing a second one soon.

"The bedroom's got plenty of space. You'll be able to manage with, say, the cot over here until..."

She looks confused. "What do you mean, cot?

You don't think..."

Oh no, she's not just a bit heavy, is she? Great. First I find out Rob's taken, but now I've insulted his wife - a potential customer - I think I can say goodbye to this deal going through. Since there's no hope of the earth swallowing me up, I just want to get this ordeal over with so I can go home.

When Rob comes back into the room, she starts laughing.

"Hey Rob, she thought we were together," she says. "God, no. He's my husband's friend. He's asked me to come along because I'm a quantity surveyor, so I could give it a check for any major faults. Even though domestic isn't really my field and he's not buying it, you don’t want to take on anything bad, do you?"

I feel a right div now. Still, it means he's probably not married. If he did have a wife or girlfriend, presumably she'd have come along to this viewing. Sometimes one person will come on their own for a first viewing if their partner can't get time off or whatever, but they'd both usually be there for the second viewing. I need to know though.

"So Mr Jones," I ask tentatively, "it'll just be your name on the lease?"

Rob smiles. Does he know why I'm asking?

"It'll be just me and Bob living here, but he's more of a silent partner," he says.

Bob. So he doesn't have a wife, he's got a boyfriend. Male or female, I'm not really bothered. All I know is he's taken and I've made a huge idiot of myself. I'm sure he knows I fancy him. Oh well, maybe I've dodged a bullet, I think. He seems to be willing to make big decisions without consulting his partner. Don't care how fit he is, I couldn't put up with someone like that.

"Well, are you sure your..." I hesitate, unsure whether to say 'boyfriend' or 'partner' and end up saying, "... your Bob wouldn't like to see the apartment before you make a decision? I'd really like both parties in a couple to be happy before they sign the contract."

The woman laughs again.

"Bob's his dummy," she explains. "One of those human punchbags people use to practise martial arts and boxing. He's living in our spare room at the moment, and love him as I do, I've told Bob he's got," she places a hand on her bump, "18 weeks left before he's got to find a new home."

"Don't worry, I think Bob'll be packing his

bags and giving you some space pretty soon," Rob says. "I'd like to take this flat, Nikki." He looks around the room, which is empty except for a bed and wardrobe. "It'll be a nice place for me and Bob. I'll stand him in the corner and he can vet any girls I bring home."

Okay... the idea of having to win the approval of a big lump of flesh-coloured rubber (the woman he was with showed me a pic of Bob on her phone, wearing one of her bras and a hat) is a bit strange to say the least, but if Rob's talking about bringing girls home, I think it's safe to say he's single.

I wonder if the thirty-two year old, single parent who's handling the lease on his flat counts as 'girls', though? He looks late twenties, thirty at most. What if he goes for little, giggly twenty-three year olds who are into Snapchat and say things like 'Totes amaze balls' all the time?

I say goodbye to them, having made the all-important appointment for him to come in and sign the contracts in the morning, and head off to collect Jamie. Even though nothing'll come of this, at least I can think I've made my first step to getting back in the game.

Still, I put my ring back on before I collect Jamie from the in-laws.

6

So, the next day, Rob came in to sign the contracts and arrange a date for moving in. As I knew he was coming, I'd taken my ring off again and blow-dried my hair instead of just letting it dry naturally as I did most other mornings. Not sure why, just because I'd fairly safely established he was available, that didn't mean I could pounce on him or anything, did it?

"Someone here to see you, Nikki," Karen called through from the showroom. "I think it's the man you've been waiting for," she added, giggling.

I looked across at her, shaking my head and narrowing my eyes to show her I didn't need her wind-ups right now and thought, would you just shut up, please? It was going to be awkward enough sorting out his contract without letting it show too much that I liked him. With the women in the shop front making silly remarks, it'd be impossible.

I led him through to what Jeanette, my mum and Christine refer to as my office, but is really just a small side room that I suspect may have been a cupboard once upon a time. Hopefully I can just get through this, forget about him and move on.

He pointed to the chair that looked like it should be for a customer, but had a stack of flat-printed cardboard folders that I'd already asked Chelsea to start folding on it and asked, "Okay, do you want me on this one?"

I inwardly groaned. Why would someone say that, unless they meant it as some kind of innuendo? I thought, he's twigged I like him and he's winding me up, isn't he? It's probably dead funny to him that this sad old woman was flirting with him at a viewing.

I shifted the folders out of the way. "Yes please, Mr Jones."

Yeah, you're not Rob anymore, I thought. Let's make you feel old and see how you like it. Still, I had to remain professional, so I offered him a drink as it was going to take best part of an hour to do what we had to do.

"Thanks. Coffee, if that's alright. Hot and strong, and I was born sweet so I don't need sugar," he answered, accompanying it with a cheesy grin, as if he knew what he was saying sounded a bit silly and he was joking with me.

"Coming right up," I replied, pausing for a second to take him in. Oh, even though he's a wind-up merchant, he's so good-looking, I thought. He'd taken off his jacket and was wearing a white T-shirt with a pair of braces. Not something I'd usually like: I think they look ridiculous on most people, but on him they seemed to emphasise his oh-so slightly defined chest. Not a muscleman, but not flabby either. Nice.

He'd been completely clean-shaven at the weekend, but today he had a couple of days' worth of stubble. Again, I've never been one for facial hair, I hate the current fashion for even young men to have big thick Father Christmas beards, but it just made him seem even more attractive.

As I nipped to the kitchen to make the drinks, I thought, why did this have to happen? Okay, Laura had a point and I have to get myself back out there and find someone one day, but why did the first one I like have to be a) a client, so he's off-limits no matter what, and b) three years younger and so hot he'll never look at me – and just to finish it, he knows I like him? I'm not sure I'm ready for this. Right, I told myself, get a grip. Just go in, be professional but cool with him, and then never bother with men ever again.

I brought the drinks in and, while I called his details up on the computer, he took a sip and said, "Ooh, that's perfect. I've been gasping all morning."

You have no idea, I thought to myself.

After forty-five minutes, we'd completed the paperwork and arranged that he'd return, once I'd set up his bank transfer and checked his references, to collect the keys to the flat.

Which he did a week later, before driving off in a rented white van to his new home.

Oh well, you often hear people say that sometimes a person comes into your life for a reason. I guess the reason Rob Jones appeared was to get me to start thinking about finding love again, before disappearing out of my life to live on the other side of town with his rubbery flatmate.

****

Laura shakes her head.

"Alright, so he didn't pull you over the desk and ravish you in the middle of the office," she says, "but why does that mean nothing can ever happen?"

"Because he's a ..." I begin saying.

Laura's having none of it.

"A client, I know, you keep saying. What I want to know is, why is that such a big problem? If you were a teacher and he was in Year 10 or something, I could see why it'd be wrong, but you're both adults, for God's sake! As long as you're not being a total stalker, the worst he could do would be say no. You keep saying you'd lose your job. Think about it, what's he going to say to Head Office?"

She affects a grave, mock-outraged tone, and says, "'One of your Lettings managers politely asked me to have a drink with her, and I'm mortally offended'? I bet he'd be made up. From the things you told me he said, I think he was trying to flirt with you, and you just couldn't see it."

I look at her, a bit doubtful.

"Do you really think, Laura? I just thought he

was winding me up."

She lets out a giggle and smiles. "Any man who says, 'Ooh, I'm gagging for it' when you give him a coffee is interested, I'm telling you, Nik."

"He didn't say 'gagging', it was 'gasping'," I correct her. "I just assumed he was really thirsty."

She laughs and points a finger towards me, with a triumphant grin. "You're not wrong there, but I reckon he wants something hot and steamy from you, and it's not coffee!"

We have to stop talking for a few minutes because Jamie's got out of bed and is wandering around upstairs. After I've tucked her back in and told her it's lights off and she's got to go to sleep, I come back down. I consider changing the subject, but if I'm honest, I'm intrigued by the idea that Rob might like me. Flattered as well – who wouldn't be? He's 29 (even though it's not on the rental agreement, I slipped in a cheeky enquiry about his date of birth, and without thinking, he just gave me it along with all of the other information I actually did need) and really nice. I look at myself in the hall mirror before coming back into the living room. I know I'm not too dreadful to look at and I wouldn't say I've really let myself go just because I've been a widow for nearly six years, but I still find it a bit hard to believe I'd be his type – unless he has a thing for tired-looking single mums.

I sit back down. Laura continues painting her toenails. I tell her that it's a nice idea to think Rob might be interested, but even if you take the view that we're adults and the client thing shouldn't matter, it's all irrelevant. He's gone. He's got a flat, so he won't be coming into the showroom to look for a place anymore. He'll just pay his rent through bank transfer and I shouldn't see him until whenever he moves out.

She screws the top back onto the bottle of polish.

"Yeah, he won't be coming into your office again, but the one big advantage of all this is that you know where he lives, don't you?" As I open my mouth to remind her yet again of the wrongness of using a client's personal details for my own interests, she says, "I know what you're going to say, Nik. No, of course you can't get his number from the files and call him, or knock at his flat, but..."

She pauses, as if she's about to reveal a stroke of genius, which actually, she is.

"If you know where he lives, then you know where his local pub is. Where the local shops are. Basically, you hang around there until you see him. Unless he's a total hermit, he's got to go for a drink or shopping at some point, hasn't he? And there's nothing at all to stop you shopping or drinking in places he might be outside of working hours."

I reach for the nail polish.

"Hmm, maybe that's not a bad idea. As long as we don't do anything too weird; we're not actively seeking him out, just hanging out in places he might be. And it would be nice to see him again. You know Laura, I do like him. I haven't felt like this, well you know how long it's been. I wouldn't want to let him go if he might like me, but I can't go freaking him out or making a fool of myself either."

After Laura's gone home, I feel a bit excited at the thought of maybe seeing Rob again. Obviously, I'm completely ignoring the question of what on earth I'll say if I see him. With any luck, inspiration will hit me like a thunderbolt at the time.

Lying in bed, I say what I always say, adding, "You do understand, don't you, love?"

I hope he would. We never talked about this sort of thing (we were in our twenties, why would we?), but I'd like to think I'd have been okay with Shaun meeting someone else if things had been the other way round.

7

One Sunday afternoon during the school holidays, I decide to talk to Jamie about Shaun. I know we gave her a bit of (not entirely true) explanation that time in the pub, but I think I'd better address it before she gets any older and genuinely confused.

I bide my time. We go for a swim. I've really missed being able to take her to the Water Babes sessions. Laura would sometimes take her when I went full time and I always felt envious when she'd tell me about it. There's no inflatables or music today, but it's still fun to splash about and great to see how confident - no, make that fearless - she is in the water.

It's one of those dull, slightly chilly days you sometimes get in August, so when we get back home, I make us both some hot chocolate. Hers is more like lukewarm chocolate milk, but she's delighted with the idea of having a grown-up 'hot' drink. We both cuddle up on the couch, hands wrapped round our mugs even though it's not really that cold. I've got some photo albums from mine and Shaun's wedding on the coffee table in front of us... and the box.

Underneath my bed, I keep a box of memories. There's all sorts of things in there: ticket stubs from gigs we went to or films we saw, interesting shells or pine cones from walks we went on, even a paper menu from Churritos that he wrote his number on when he asked me to call him again after our first date. I always hoped Shaun and I would root through them in our old age and share happy memories, but at least they'll be able to show the daughter he never met a bit about what her dad was like.

Jamie asks if she can watch Peppa Pig on my tablet, but I reckon it's time to do this now or I'll chicken out.

"Tell you what love, you can do that later. I want to talk to you about something first. Something really important."

She may be a couple of months away from

being five years old, but my Jamie is sharper than some adults I've met. She immediately senses the seriousness of my tone.

"Am I in trouble, Mummy?"

I put my arm round her. "No, not at all, love. It's just that I really want you to listen to what I'm going to say. I wanted to tell you about your daddy."

She looks excited. "Is he coming back from Heaven?"

I take a deep breath. This might be harder than I thought, not that I expected it to be easy.

"No," I tell her. "Remember, Grandad said your daddy can't come back, ever. I wish every day that he could come back because," I stop for a couple of seconds to compose myself. I'm getting a bit wobbly already but I've got to keep myself together, "I loved him a lot. More than anything. As much as I love you. I wish he was here so he could take you to Water Babes and watch Peppa Pig with you."

It's no good. A tear escapes, but I wipe it away as quickly as I can, hoping she won't see.

"So was my Daddy a nice man, then?" she asks.

I sigh. How I am supposed to do this and not end up a blubbering wreck? Deep breath again.

"Oh love, he was the best man in the world. He'd always make me laugh and he'd give me great big hugs, and I know he'd have done exactly the same for you."

I open the photo album and show her pictures of our wedding and honeymoon. They distract her somewhat and allow me to recover. I start looking through the memory box. The box of confetti someone brought to throw over us as we left the registry office has split open, leaving little hearts and horseshoes dotted around the box. I smile. In fact, whenever I get this box out to look through, I can usually feel some comfort in the reminders of the good times we had. There's only one thing I never get out: the keyring with the keys to his Pulsar on it. The car was a write off, but the police recovered those and returned them to me. I'd never throw them away because he loved that car so much but I can't even touch them, it's too painful.

After a while, even though Peppa Pig drives me nuts, I think I'd be quite glad to see her, so I put the box and album on the stairs ready to go up later. Actually, I don't think that went too badly. Okay, I didn’t get as far as discussing death - I didn't want to, she's still only four - but she fully understands that although her dad's not here, he was a real person. She knows what he looked like and what he did.

As I'm finding the episode she wants, Jamie stuns me with a question.

"Mummy, will I ever get a new daddy? Ava-Grace has got one."

I can't be disloyal to Shaun. "No love, you only ever get one daddy."

"But she has, Mummy. She goes to her old daddy's house on Saturday but her new daddy lives with her mummy and he watches Peppa Pig with her. If my daddy can't come back from Heaven, maybe one day I'll get a new daddy. Will I?"

I'm surprised by that, but I suppose I shouldn't be. Children can sometimes accept some of life's changes a lot more easily than adults. Since I've been wondering about whether I could or should look for a relationship, the effect it might have on my daughter has always been a huge concern.

Sounds like she'd actually like to have someone who could do things a dad does... but is that person Rob Jones? Even if I manage to spot him in his local pub or wherever, and even if it's true that he actually was interested in me, he could still run a mile when he finds out I'm a widow with a child. People always use the word 'baggage' to describe this situation. Jamie's not baggage, she's a blessing and if I can ever meet the right man, he'd understand that – but there are a lot of men out there who wouldn't feel the same way.

I have two choices: either sit here and do nothing, or find out what kind of man Rob is.

8

Why didn't I just sit there and do nothing?

For the last fortnight, Laura and I have spent three nights a week investigating the pubs in the vicinity of Rob's flat. And we haven't seen him once.

The first night, we went for the one closest to his flat, assuming that'd be the one he'd choose. Big mistake. Proper old man's pub. There wasn't a soul in there aged under 150. They were even playing that weird game where you shove matchsticks in holes on a board that I remember being shown when I was at school – and even that was in a module about how the Victorians had to make their own fun!

Still, we thought we'd hang around for one drink at least, to wait and see if he might show up; although I was starting to think I could go off him if he liked this sort of place. The landlord huffed when I asked for a Diet Coke (if we were going to be snooping round pubs all night, I didn't want to be hammered when or if I eventually did see Rob) and then refused to serve Laura a pint, eventually giving her it in two half-pint glasses when she threatened to report him to Judge Rinder for being sexist.

We necked our drinks as quickly as we could, having decided this definitely *wasn't* Rob's kind of place, as if we knew anything about him.

Sitting in the fourth pub we'd tried, the one we seemed to like best (or just disliked least), we reasoned that, if it wasn't either full of people who could remember the Battle of Waterloo or full of screaming kids who should have gone to bed hours ago, it might be the one Rob would pick when he came out for a... whatever he drinks.

"Oh sod it, I'm having a wine next time. I've had enough of being sober. You want one?" I ask her. She nods, as she picks up her cider with three inches left in it and downs it in one.

After I've come back from the bar, I take a large gulp before letting out an exasperated sigh.

"This is a total waste of time. I know Christine and Mum don't mind babysitting, but I'm running out of lies to invent to say where I've been. Mum's already said it's a bit weird I'm suddenly going out so much."

Laura swings back and stares at me. Maybe this should be her last drink.

"What's wrong with saying you're with me?" she says, clearly a bit tipsy.

"Nothing, but if I tell them I'm having a drink with you, they'll wonder why I can't just buy a couple of bottles of wine and have you round at mine like we usually do. I'm pretending to see films and other things and to be honest, Laura, I'm starting to wonder what's the point? This is pathetic when you think about it. What am I, some schoolkid hanging around to see if the boy she fancies gets on the same bus or something? Even if he did like me, I bet he's forgotten about me by now."

Laura shrugs. She sounds a bit cheesed off.

"Okay, I was just trying to help. We don't need to bother any more, we can just stay in and have no chance of meeting anyone at all."

I take another glug of my wine and think that

wouldn't be a bad thing. I do feel pretty stupid, spending all my evenings chasing round after someone who won't even remember what I look like - and that's if he ever cared in the first place.

"He probably doesn't even drink. I know we're a pair of winos when we get together, but if he's got that dummy for boxing practice, he's probably one of those 'my body is a temple' types," I say, draining my glass and reaching for my jacket.

Laura laughs. "Yeah, and didn't you say they took a picture of that dummy wearing a hat and his mate's wife's bra? Does that sound like the sort of thing people do after a nice cup of tea? Nik, that is a man who is not afraid to have a drink. We just need to find out where the hell he does it... and then you can start worshipping that temple," she says, jiggling her hips back and forward. I know she's my mate, but she's such dirty mare sometimes.

"Well it's probably at home, like when we have a drink, isn't it? We've already established that I can't go hassling him there and frankly, I've had enough of lurking around this neighbourhood on the one-in-a-million off chance that I'll be in the same place at the same time as a customer I had a more than two weeks ago. I give in. Let's go home."

During the next week at work, I decide to do something that worked for me before. Or at least, it worked once, and I wasn't trying to make anything happen. Instead of reading a book on my lunch break or just working through (things have gone a bit quiet recently, so it really doesn't matter much if I take the full hour), I head round to the park. The place where I met Shaun. I was just sitting minding my own business (well, I was making guesses about everyone else's, but I don't think anyone ever realised) and the love of my life came to me. Maybe if I get myself out there, instead of lurking around in crappy pubs waiting for one particular man to notice me, I could meet someone.

The trouble is, when I met Shaun I was eleven years younger. Sitting on the common, surrounded by what look like teenagers but they can't all be (I know, they always say that's one of the signs you're getting old, when police officers, doctors and basically everyone start looking young to you), I just feel like I don't belong there. I finish my salad, put my lunchbox back in my bag and head back to the office.

So that's it. I let Rob slip away, I can't go chasing after any other decent blokes who might come in (and there hasn't been anyone in his league since) to the showroom for the same reason I never chased Rob... and my days of clubbing and being able to pull in a bar, or even in the park, are long gone. I may as well give up and just accept that it's just me and Jamie forever.

Then, just to make my day even worse, Jeanette calls me in for a meeting. She calls it an Interface Update Situation, so I guess she's been reading another management textbook. Basically, she's aware things have slowed down a bit in Lettings, and she wants me to see what I can do to get things moving again.

"I'll have a think, Jeanette. I don't want to let you down after you gave me this chance. I'll wear that T-shirt again if I have to – hell, I'll run down the high street wearing only a sash saying 'Crostons Lettings' if it gets people to notice us."

Jeanette smiles. "Well, I'm not sure our Lettings manager getting arrested is quite the publicity Head Office have in mind, but see what you can do. We could really do with doubling the current revenue from rental commissions in the next quarter."

Back at my desk, I jot a few ideas on my notepad. T-shirt? Easy. Still got it in my desk drawer. Mailshot all the terraced houses and flats, or all the likely properties in the area? Fine, I can design a flyer in ten minutes and get them distributed no problem. There's got to be something else I can do, though...

While I'm waiting for a more dynamic idea to hit me, I spend the next half hour approaching everyone who comes in to look at properties for sale to ask if they've got any need to rent somewhere if they're stuck in a chain. It doesn't result in anything, so I'm about to set off to do a viewing when a woman in her fifties pushes the showroom door angrily. She marches up to Karen's desk and growls, "Who deals with the rental properties?"

Okay, she seems a bit uptight, but if it could be a lead she can be as narky as she wants, I think. I walk over to where she's standing and say, "Good afternoon, Madam. I'm Nikki Dunne, Lettings manager. How can..."

She doesn't let me finish, or want to shake the hand I've extended.

"I don't care who you are, love," she says, "I live next door to one of your tenants and they're a bloody nightmare. Why haven't you done anything about it?"

I think I know who she means. About two months ago, we let a three bedroom house to a family. They had all the usual references, but I can only assume their previous landlord lied and gave them a good one just so they could be rid of them. I've already had several phone calls complaining about their dogs barking excessively and loud music playing into the night. Only last week, I sent the tenants a letter warning them that they were in breach of their contract and if things didn't improve, we had the right to evict them.

I can't assume though, so I ask the woman which house she means. When she confirms it is the one I already knew about, I tell her I have already given them a warning, but her complaint now means I can organise an eviction and they'll be gone within two weeks.

This doesn't satisfy the woman.

"Two bloody weeks? I want them out now! I haven't slept properly since they arrived and they keep throwing dirty nappies into my yard. Get them out now!"

"I'm sorry Madam, it's not as simple as that. We have to..."

"Don't give me that! You'd move a lot quicker if it was one of the posh flats by the docks, wouldn't you? Just 'cause I live in a terrace in a rough area, you don't care. It used to be a nice road and people like them are ruining it.

Sort it out!"

"Madam, I promise where the property is has no bearing on the situation. I'll try to..."

Then, maybe because she hasn't had much sleep, maybe because she's seeing red and thinking I don't want to help her (which I do, I'd hate to be in her shoes, but I have to observe the procedures), she steps forwards and shoves me with the palm of her hand.

"I haven't slept in a sodding week and you don't care, do you? My husband works nights and he's got those dogs barking all day, but that doesn't matter to you, does it?"

Although I'm shocked, I take a step backwards, away from her and say, "Look. I know you're angry but there's no need for that. Just calm down, right?"

She steps towards me, cornering me by a freestanding column display of property pictures. Still furious, she shoves me again, this time slamming me into the display.

"I won't bloody calm down! I've had enough and I'm not going 'til you get something done!"

"You're not going anywhere, that's true," shouts Jeanette, who's come out of her office to see what's going on and is standing over the door. "Karen, call the police. You can't come in here shouting the odds and assaulting my staff."

Then, as if the realisation of what she's done hits her, the woman changes completely. She seems to shrink a little as her anger is replaced by fear and embarrassment. She puts one hand over her mouth and tries to reach out to me with the other, but I step away.

"Oh my God, I am so sorry," she says in a terrified voice. "I didn't mean that, I've never done anything like that in my life. They just pushed me over the edge. It's every day, and we can't sleep. The only times I see my husband we're yelling at each other 'cause we're so tired, and now I've done this..." She stops talking and gives in to sobbing.

She sits down on the chair in front of Karen's desk. "Oh God, what am I going to get for this?" She looks across at me. "Honestly, love, I didn't... you're not hurt, are you?"

I am a bit hurt, actually. My right shoulder's really sore from where it hit the display, but as I look at this woman, reduced to weeping in the middle of an estate agency showroom, terrified of an assault charge, I'm not overly concerned about my injuries.

I look across at Karen, then Jeanette.

"Karen, instead of ringing the police, could you rearrange my 2.45 viewing, please? Jeanette, could we take this into your office? I don't think this should be done out on the shop floor."

Suddenly, as if I'm the boss and Jeanette is my employee, she nods and the three of us head into her room.

After half an hour of discussion, I say I'm prepared to accept the woman's profuse (and they are, I really don't think she's the kind of person to do that sort of thing normally) apologies and that I'm happy enough not to press charges or take the matter any further – as long as she doesn't come back. I assure her the tenants will be gone as soon as I can arrange it.

"Well, that's all well and good, but are you okay, Nikki?" Jeanette asks me when the woman has gone.

I flex my right arm a little.

"It hurts when I do this," I tell her. "I'll sleep on it and see how it is in the morning. I know people might say I should have got the police in, but you could see that woman. She was a decent person who's been driven mad. Who knows what any of us would do if we were pushed to the limit? If she'd got arrested that would have been one more nightmare for her, and it wouldn't make my shoulder any better."

Jeanette pats me on the shoulder, stopping when I give a little whimper of pain.

"Well, you're a better woman than me, Nikki. I don't think I'd be as forgiving as you. But thanks. It wouldn't have been particularly good publicity to have people discussing bad tenants in a Crostons property in court."

She holds the door of her office open. "Right then, off you go. I think you should take the rest of the day off to recuperate."

9

Since the day I found out Jamie was going to arrive, everyone around me promised I'd never have to feel alone. Obviously, I've had family around to do things like babysitting if I needed a break or night out, and both my mum and Christine are often popping by with some dress, book or other little item they've spotted while out shopping. Between family, my recent increase in salary and the usual child credits most parents get, I manage okay financially, and I know there's always someone I can ask for help with most things.

But that doesn't mean there haven't been times when I wished Shaun could have been there: getting up for night feeds when she was tiny, someone else to share the delight of seeing her take her first steps or witness her first smile... and today's another one of those milestones.

"Give me a big smile, Jay!"

Sorry, but I'm taking *those* pictures. The ones every childless person gets sick to the back teeth of in the first week of every September. Jamie looks adorable in her grey pinafore with a little bow detail on each of the pockets, with a white blouse and pillar-box red cardi.

She comes running up to me from where she's been posing at the end of the hall (the most presentable bit of our house because it's nothing but bare walls and laminate floor) and grabs at my arm, wanting to see the pictures on my phone.

"Oh sh...", I say, stopping myself from giving the most natural reaction to the stabbing pain in my shoulder. "Don't do that, love. You know Mummy's arm still hurts after that sign fell on me at work."

Obviously, I didn't tell Jamie I'd been attacked by a customer, even if they were really sorry afterwards. I wouldn't want her to think that kind of thing can happen to me at work. Anyway, what seems to bother her more is that since I hurt my shoulder, it's been hard to help her out of the bath or open a tin of beans without whimpering, and as for playing catch in the park – forget it.

"Mummy, you should go to the doctor and get them to make it better," she grumbles, before readjusting her socks.

True, maybe I should, I think to myself. It has been a few weeks since it happened and it isn't feeling any better. Jeanette's allowed me to come to work a little later today so I could take Jamie to school on her first day, but I'm wondering if I could get this looked at as well before I go to work.

After a couple of quick phone calls, I've arranged to see my GP at 9.45. I don't have any appointments booked in, and I think Jeanette feels that since my injury happened on company time, Crostons kind of owes me.

"So, basically I've damaged this thing in my shoulder called the rotator cuff," I tell her when I arrive at the showroom. It's nearly 11 o'clock by now because the doctors were running late and I didn't get seen 'til 10.15 but, like I said, maybe she doesn't feel she can complain too much about it in case I felt like running to one of those ambulance-chasing call centres you see advertised all the time. "They've given me a sheet of exercises to do, and they've suggested things like swimming or aquarobics."

"Glad to hear it shouldn't be anything too serious, Nikki," Jeanette replies. She may be my boss, but she is a decent person. I think she is genuinely concerned about me, and not just the idea of avoiding a lawsuit. "If we can help you in any way, just say."

Hmm, I think. This could be the time to ask. I reach around in my bag and pull out the leaflet the doctor gave me.

"Well," I begin, "there is something I wouldn't mind doing, if it's okay. There's these Aqua Therapy classes on at the leisure centre. The doctor reckons they can really help, but they're on at 12 midday on Tuesdays. If I made up the time, could I take two hours for lunch once a week, so I could get there and back?"

"No problem at all, Nikki," she says. "I just want you back to full strength. And there's no need to make the time up, for, shall we say eight weeks? Hopefully that'll be enough to sort you out."

Nice one, I think as I turn back to my room to start working through my messages. Obviously, what I want most is to get this shoulder sorted, but I've really missed going to Water Babes with Jamie. Maybe this'll be like that, but for adults.

"She's bricking it in case you sue," Laura says as the barista shouts that our order's ready. I get up and collect our coffees and panini. It drives me nuts when people says paninis, you don't say paparazzis do you? Shaun always used to laugh at me, saying my English Literature with World Linguistics degree obviously qualified me to be a grammar Nazi in several languages, because I hate it when people don't say 'chorizo' correctly either.

Anyway, I bring our tray over and she goes on, while cutting her panino (told you) in half.

"You should have held out for a whole afternoon off once a week. That way, you could have done your aquaphysio thing, then gone for a massage afterwards. You're too nice, Nik."

Damn. That does actually sound good... and I might have been able to swing it because Jeanette (or at least the company) probably are a little bit wary of legal action. Still, the extra hour off's not bad. If it doesn't get better, I could always press for the massage later.

"It's fine," I tell her. "As long as it sorts me out, that's all I want. Then when I'm better, I'll be back up to speed at work, win Lottings Manager of the Quarter and treat myself to a massage to celebrate!"

Laura, about to take a bite, lowers her hand. Then she says nothing but just looks at me, open-mouthed, for a second.

"Nik, this is bad. I mean, I know you're not exactly..."

I can see her struggling for a polite way to finish the sentence without saying I'm basically a boring mum with no sense of adventure. I can't help it. I'm just not a loud, outgoing character like her. She's talked herself into (and out of) God knows how many situations and always seems to come out smiling. I'm just not like that. Call me a wuss if you want, but the thought of taking any risk bigger than changing my lunch order brings me out in a rash and it might sound boring, especially to someone like her, but the thought of even being considered for a regional award at work would make my year.

"You?" I finish it for her. "We can't all be like you, Laura. Some of us are... well, it wouldn't do for us all to be the same, would it?"

"I didn't mean anything by it, Nik," she says. "All I meant was that if winning a bottle of Costco bubbly and having your back pummelled by some bored schoolkid on work experience are your life goals, then we have got to get you a man." She gives her coffee another stir, before saying quietly, "Come on, have a look around. Anyone in here you like the look of?"

I don't know why, maybe just to stop her going on about it, I cast my eyes around the coffee shop.

"No. No-one," I reply firmly, before picking up my cheese and ham (I might risk the odd change in my choice of coffee - going all the way from cappuccino to a flat white once - but I don't think I've ever deviated from my go-to sandwich filling) sandwich and taking a bite. "Now, can we drop it and talk about something else? I'd just like us to have a nice lunch before it goes cold."

"I wouldn't worry about a bloody sandwich when the rest of your life's going cold, Nik," she says. "Okay, your job's important, I get that. But, to be honest," she hesitates, "sometimes you do seem a bit old before your time. You're still young enough to have a life, but it seems like you just don't want to sometimes. Even when you actually showed an interest in that bloke from work a while back, you wouldn't go after him."

I sigh. I'm a bit pissed off with her. This is like that night at my house when she told me to start moving on from Shaun. I don't want to get into an argument here, in the middle of a café and then have to go back to work seething with annoyance over things I didn't think to say at the time, so I stare at my half-finished lunch on the table in front of me.

Cheese and ham. What I always have. Same thing for years. Why don't I ever order a different sandwich? It's not as though I've ever tried something else and didn't like it, I just always go for the same thing.

Because it's easy and I know what I'm going to get.

She's right, isn't she? I am afraid to move on, to have fun, to admit that Shaun's gone... and that if I want to feel that kind of love again, it would have to mean allowing someone new into my world. My closed, safe, lonely world.

She can see I'm upset. She puts a hand out towards me.

"I'm sorry. I've done it again, haven't I? Me and my big mouth. I didn't mean it. Just 'cause I'm a..."

"No, it's okay Laura," I interrupt. "You're right. I wish I had said something to that Rob now, but it's too late, isn't it? I am nervous about finding someone else. What if no-one's interested?"

She edges off her chair, a little closer to me. "You're not a hundred years old, Nik. You still look good. Okay, you could do with a bit of a makeover, but I'll help you with that," she says, ignoring my slightly offended frown, "and you'll soon be beating them off with a stick!"

As I ease my jacket off (even doing that's painful) when I get back to work, I once again catch sight of my face in the mirror in the office cloakroom. I'm still not sure this is a good idea. I'm okay to look at: not amazing, but at least the mirror hasn't smashed. No, what I'm really worried about is having the confidence to go on dates – if I get asked on any, because I'd never be able to ask a man for one. I would never have got talking to Shaun if he hadn't approached me, and that was when I was younger and less wrinkly than I am now. Still, if I don't start putting myself out there again, I'm going to be on my own forever.

10

"Okay if I head off now, Jeanette?"

"Sure. Hope it goes well. See you in a bit," she calls from inside her office.

I've got my first Aqua Therapy session today and I have to admit, I'm looking forward to it in a strange sort of way. Obviously, I'm hoping it'll make my shoulder feel a bit better, but also, even though it's not designed to be fun, going out to the pool in the middle of my working day feels a bit naughty.

As I park up at the leisure centre, I consider that idea. Coming out for treatment for an injury, that my boss knows all about and has granted permission for, is as naughty as I ever get.

I frown at myself in my pull-down mirror. Laura's got a point. I'm boring. Dull. A real goody-goody. I mean, I never sagged off school even once – hell, I didn't even miss any lectures at uni. In fact, one of the biggest reasons anyone knew who I was while I was at uni was they knew I'd have turned up to the 9am lecture that they missed because they'd been out 'til 4 the night before and they could see me and ask for 'Nikki Notes'. And all of that was before I even met Shaun, so it's not even as though I can say I only became a sad old woman since I've been widowed.

Sod it. I'm going to treat myself to a coffee in the cafe after this and just tell Jeanette the session overran. And while I'm at it, I can start thinking of ways to get out there and start living again.

When I used to bring Jamie here for Water Babes, I'd use one of the double-sized changing rooms but today, since it's just me, I go for one of the tiny cubicles. A decision I regret when I get a stabbing pain through my shoulder as I try to yank my costume up over my body and bang my elbow on the wall as I try to get it on. I've got one of those costumes with a skirt attached because I feel a lot more confident in it. When I used to have a regular one, I always felt like I was walking round in my knickers. And of course, it's a handy cover up for those areas I don’t give a huge amount of attention to anymore, if you know what I mean. Let’s just say it’s not so much a dainty landing strip, more of a bush trail.

At the poolside, I sit under a fake palm tree and size up the other people who’ve come to the session: mostly older people, both men and women, probably referred by their doctors because it might help with their arthritis or something. I think it'd be fair to say I'm probably the only person there on their lunch hour.

"Okay, ladies and gents, hop in and let's get started." The instructor's a woman, maybe late twenties. She's intensely jolly, seeming unable to stand still, and pronounces every word as though she's telling you you've won the lottery.

"Right, you know what I've got to ask: is anybody pregnant?" she says, grinning.

I guess this is a routine health and safety thing, and it looks as though it's a running joke every week for a couple of the class, especially the men, to laugh and raise their hand. Then, the instructor scans around the room to see me, where I've positioned myself at the edge of the group. As I'm the only person in the room for whom it could be an actual possibility, she looks at me with an expression that says, 'Well?'

"Oh, don't worry, not a hope in hell," I answer, a little more grumpily than I should have.

It's not her fault, she's got to ask that. After all, she knows nothing about my life. For all she knows, I could have a sex-mad husband and be freshly knocked-up as a result of one of our regular shag-marathons.

The class begins. It's mostly doing stretches underwater to gentle music. It's quite nice, actually. With my shoulder under the water, it doesn't hurt at all when I move it. Some of the other people talk to each other while they exercise, but I don't try to get involved in their conversations. Not just because they're older and I might not know what to say, but I'm actually enjoying drifting away into my own little world. As long as I watch what the instructor's doing, I don't even have to listen too carefully; instead, I can just let my head go while my mind and body relax.

At the end of the session, the instructor asks me to wait for a minute so she can speak to me about my reasons for coming. I don't tell her I'm an estate agent who got assaulted by a customer: given what people tend to think of us, she'd probably find it funny. Instead, I say something similar to what I told Jamie. While I'm standing in my wet costume talking to her, I can see what's going on in the full-size training pool on the other side of a glass partition.

"So, the first thing you'd do in this situation is throw the person a buoyancy aid. They are stationed at all sides of the pool. Unravel the rope, then use an underarm motion with whichever hand you write with, holding the rope with the other hand. Right, who wants to try? Nathan? Go on, show me."

A group of about four young people, all wearing blue shorts and yellow T-shirts with 'Trainee Lifeguard' on the back, are listening to a handsome, tall man wearing glasses with the same blue shorts, only his T-shirt is red, and would presumably have 'Lifeguard Instructor' on the back instead.

Well, well, well... Rob Jones. We meet again.

I had no idea he worked here. His payslips were just standard council ones, with no indication of what his job was. He could have been anything; turns out he's a lifeguard.

I hover for a few seconds, drinking in the sight of his chest in that T-shirt. Then my eyes move down to his legs. Of course, I've never seen him in shorts before. His calves are muscular without being too thick, and he's got just the right amount of leg-hair: masculine but not gorilla-like.

This has got to be fate, hasn't it? If it wasn't for hurting my shoulder, I'd never have been here at this time of day, and I'd never have seen him again. Right, I have *got* to do something about it this time and not let him go. Maybe he doesn't like me, maybe he's found someone else since he mentioned bringing girls home at the viewing, but whatever happens, I'm not going to lose him because I sat there and did nothing.

After a few more seconds of taking in his body (ooh, he's turned round now, nice bum as well) I look down at myself. I have to hide, quick! I look... well, I look the way anyone looks after an hour in a swimming pool. My hair's soaked, straggly and I must stink of chlorine.

I turn and scurry back to my locker as fast as I dare on the wet floor, grab my stuff and shut myself in a cubicle. Good. I don't think he saw me.

Once I've got the protection of the walls around me, I relax a little. I know where I can find him now, and it's in a place where I'll be able to come for the next seven weeks!

It's not that simple though, is it? The negative side of my mind, the side that always tells me to stay back, not make a fool of myself and just get cheese and ham again because it's easier, raises a couple of problems. Fine, you know where he is on a Tuesday. Doesn't change anything. He's not able to stop and talk to you even if he wants to, he'll be busy training up his students. And for the same reason you weren't able to approach him, there's probably some rule in the Lifeguard's Code of Practice stating that they can't chat up people who come for a swim.

Well, maybe not, I think. But there's got to be something I can do. I've got seven weeks to make contact with him. Just got to think of how... but first, I'm going to start have my first bit of naughtiness by having a coffee and going back to work a little bit late. I've got to be allowed a bit of time for lunch, haven't I? And who knows, I might see Rob while I'm sitting there. I wonder if I can sip a cappuccino in a seductive way if he walks by? At least I'm on my own. I've never been ashamed of Jamie, but I guess it wouldn't create the best impression if the first time he sees me in ages is while I'm telling her not to blow bubbles in her milkshake and wiping blobs of ketchup off the table.

I smooth my hair one last time (not that it

does a lot of good, I still look a mess. Maybe I shouldn't do this) and plonk my bag of wet swimming gear on a chair in the café. Come on Nikki, it's time to get back in the game.

Just hope I don't go out in the first round.

11

He didn't come into the café. I sat there, doing my best to look all sultry, seaswept and desirable, when in reality I probably just looked less Little Mermaid, more sea urchin. All I got was stuck in a traffic jam on the way back and a rather pointed, "Nice to see you back," from Jeanette when I tried to sneak past her office when I got in at nearly half past two.

Hmm. I'd better not take the piss with the extra time off again, I thought. Being naughty's only okay if you've really got the balls for it. And you don't need your job.

So, it's Tuesday again and time for my next Aqua Therapy. I'm wondering what I can do this time. Usually, or at least back in the day when I was looking for someone, if I was on the pull I'd put on a really good outfit and make sure my make-up was on point. Can't really do either of those things here, can I? Rob's seen me dressed, but only in the straight skirt and blouse I wear for work. Crostons has a uniform policy of pale blue blouse and navy straight skirt, so my clothes don't give away much about my personality. Or show my (not too bad, a little bit of mummy-tummy but I haven't let myself go completely) figure off particularly well.

Swimming costumes, on the other hand, show off a bit too much figure considering I hardly know him. They're all wet and clingy, for a start. You've got to be perfect to feel completely body-confident walking around once you've been in the water. Also, I know the skirt cozzie's a must for me, but I just hope he doesn't know they pretty much only sell them in 'old lady' shops – you know, the kind of place where they do those elasticated trousers and floor-length nighties.

I know because I went with my mum once, alright? I know I'm not Lady Gaga, but my dress sense isn't that old yet.

Perhaps I need to try to see him before I get into the water.

Once I've got changed into my costume, but before I've entered the water and spoilt everything, I go for a little wander around to the training pool. I can see some lanes dividing one half of the pool down its length, and about twenty of those rectangular floats on the water at the shallow end. They must have had a school group in.

About halfway down the pool, there's a door. I guess that it's a store cupboard which has been opened to get all the floats out. Someone's in there, moving stuff around. As I'm a reasonable enough distance away, I wait and see if it's him.

From the other side of the partition, I can hear the music's begun. I'd better go and join the Aqua Therapy class. Just as I'm about to turn, the store cupboard door opens wide and Rob comes out.

He uses a large net to pull in most of the floats before spotting me out of the corner of his eye.

"Aqua's in the other pool," he says absently, before noticing that it's me. He stops what he's doing and walks towards me. This is good, at least he's remembered me. Is he going to still know my name though?

"Hello. You're Nikki from the rental office, aren't you?"

Yayyy!!!!

"Fancy seeing you here. Erm, you do know you can't swim right now, though? I've got a training session on now, you see I train the new lifeguards, and there's old folks aqua on in the other pool."

Old folks aqua. Great.

Suddenly, it doesn't really matter that my hair's not messed up yet, I haven't showered my make-up off and my costume's not clinging mercilessly to every lump and bump. What's the point in any of it when you're the kind of person who does 'old folks aqua'?

My answer's part defensive, part apologetic.

"Well, it's not only for old people," I begin. "My doctor told me about it after I got an injury. I know it's mostly older people, but anyone can go."

His face is sympathetic. By now, I expect this is just basic politeness that a member of staff has to show to a customer, not that he cares anything about me.

"Oh no, what happened? Someone hit the back of your car or something?"

I suppose I should be grateful he didn't ask if I had rheumatism or a hip replacement, he obviously thinks I'm such an old biddy.

"No, it was something at work." No matter how ancient he obviously thinks I am, or how disappointed I feel, I could still stand there forever, trying to get a look at his eyes and definitely getting a look at that chest. I know some women complain about men looking only at their chest, but with someone of his height, I don't really have a lot of choice unless I want to risk doing my neck in as well as my shoulder.

"Well, I'd better go and join the old folks," I say with a defeated tone in my voice.

"Good to see you again," he says, again just something we all say out of politeness. "Hey, don't let them turn you. Say no to the Fisherman's Friends and tartan slippers! Bye now."

He walks round to the other side of the pool, where the same four trainee lifeguards as last week are waiting. As I head to where my class is just starting, I hear him say, "Very funny, Josh. That'd be nice, but no. We're going to practise mouth-to-mouth on this dummy instead."

Last week, I was able to relax during the class and allow my thoughts to wander. This week, my mind's racing after that little comment. What on earth did that mean? The negative side that always wants to think the worst says all the boy meant was could he practise mouth-to-mouth on one of the girls in the class, or maybe he offered an invitation to Rob... but for once, my positive side's determined to have her say as well.

Come on, Nikki, believe in yourself for once. That Josh saw you and Rob talking and asked if he'd be doing mouth-to-mouth on YOU! Not only that, but Rob said, 'That'd be nice'! He's interested, or at least he doesn't completely hate you. Maybe he doesn't even think you're really old. After all, he did talk about the old folks as 'them', as if I wasn't one of them.

When I've got my clothes back on, it's time to get back to work. No hanging around having a coffee this week. I don't want Jeanette getting annoyed and withdrawing her previous offer. As I reach the foyer of the leisure centre, I get a surprise.

He's there. Standing by the exit. There's only one way out of the place, so it's impossible to leave without seeing him. I shoot back into the toilets.

My hair's wet, but it's brushed and tidied enough to be presentable for the afternoon at work once it's dried. I fumble in my makeup bag and hastily apply some eyeshadow and lip colour. Then I reach into the zip pocket of my handbag and find my earrings. I was going to put them back in when I'd got to work, but...

Actually, maybe not. I leave one earring in my bag, then walk out with the other one concealed in my palm. I approach the door, where he's still standing, as calmly as possible.

"Hello Rob. Well, I think I'm okay. I haven't been hit with a mad urge to go home and watch 'Countdown'."

He smiles. "Glad to hear it. Look, will you do me a favour? Don't tell them I called it 'old folks aqua,' will you? I didn't mean it like that, but I don't want anyone taking it the wrong way. It's just, well, most of the people who are able to do a class in the middle of the day tend to be retired."

I hope my face isn't giving anything away, but I'm thinking, I'd take anything anyway from you, Rob Jones.

God, I'm starting to sound like Laura.

"No problem," I say, "I'm just glad you don't think I'm one of them."

Right. Enough small talk. Go for it.

"Erm, Rob, do you have a lost property

department or anything here? I've lost one of my earrings. This is the other one," I say, showing him the one I'm carrying. "I can leave my number, and if it turns up..."

Alright, you don't need to tell me. It's pretty tacky and desperate, but I couldn't think of anything better on the spur of the moment. Still, if it's the only way I've got of giving him my number, I'll just have to do it.

"Sure," he says. "Here, let me take your details down."

I feel as silly and giggly as I'm told I was the first time he came into the showroom as he leads me over to the reception cubicle. I stand at the front window while he goes through the 'Staff Only' door, stands behind the receptionist and introduces me to her.

"Sharon, this is Nikki. She's the agent who sorted my flat out. The one who thought Bob was my fella."

He's been talking about me? Okay, the things he's said make me sound a bit daft, but I'll take what I can get.

"Anyway, Sharon'll take your details and we'll let you know if it shows up. See you next week then," he says, before heading through another 'Staff Only' door and out of sight.

I look down at where Sharon's already written today's date and 'lost earring' in the lost property book. She looks up at me and asks, "Is it Miss or Mrs?"

Oh. Obviously, I'm not wearing my ring now because I've just been swimming, but I'm still not brave enough to take it off full time. I've started going without it when I do things like the shopping or more frequently at work, but I still haven't wanted to face going round to see my mum without it, and certainly not Shaun's parents. I don't know what they'd say.

As for how I'd refer to myself, well, this is the first time I've had to do this. At any time I've been asked over the last six years, I've had no hesitation whatsoever. I've always called myself Mrs Dunne, because as far as I'm concerned, my marriage didn't end, it was Shaun's life that ended. But if I want to think about meeting someone new, won't everyone just think I'm unavailable if I introduce myself as 'Mrs' all the time?

I swallow and brace myself.

"Ms," I answer. "Ms Nicola Dunne."

12

I have to do some weekend work on a rota, but every few Sundays we go round to my mum's for Sunday dinner. Yes, dinner. Not lunch, even though we eat it at 2 o'clock and I refer to the midday meal as lunch every other day of the week. Lunch is a sandwich and a bag of popcorn; I think my mum's Yorkshire puddings deserve a bit more respect.

Anyway, after we've washed up, we plonk ourselves in front of the telly. She scans through the guide to see if there's anything worth watching, and ends up hitting the 'Subtitles' button. I thought I was hopeless with technology: Mum's only 64, but her ability to get on board with new developments seemed to stop with the first Michael Buble CD.

After she's said, "What's bloody wrong with

you? I don't want subtitles, just tell me what's on Channel 5!" for the third time, I put my hand out for the remote, get rid of the subtitles and find a kids' film on ITV2 that I know Jamie's already seen, but she won't mind. Once I know she's firmly gripped in one animated cat's struggle to do... whatever it is, I reckon it's time to have the conversation I've been building myself up to for the last couple of days.

I don't know why I'm so nervous about this. I shouldn't even be nervous at all. I'm 32 years old, but I'm acting like a teenager who has to ask their mum if they can stay out half an hour later. It's no-one else's business if I want to start looking for a man... except I suppose in my circumstances, that's not really the case, is it?

It's Jamie's business, for a start. Obviously, she's the child and I'm the adult, she's not going to dictate every aspect of my life, but this is one aspect she definitely has some sway over. It's not like when I was younger and could just go on a date and see where it went: now, if I meet someone, I have to ask myself, would I happy for this person to be around my child?

Then of course, there's the fact that I might be single, but as a widow I'm far from being a completely free agent. There's the grandparents. Shaun might be gone, but his parents are a huge part of Jamie's life – and I'm happy that they are, but how will they feel if one day I introduce a new man to them? If they see him playing with Jamie the way Shaun was never able to? What if they automatically hate anyone I ever meet because he's not their son?

I'm not even sure what my own mum will think. After Dad died, she went on with her life in terms of still going to work and seeing her friends, but she hasn't had any other men in her life. Or at least if she has, I've known nothing about it, and I don't think she'd keep that from me. As an adult, I was hardly going to snarl, 'You're not my real dad!' at any boyfriend of hers, was I? I always put it down to the idea that she was just really devoted to Dad, and didn't want anyone else.

She'd married an older man, so I guess she was always prepared for the idea of him dying first. I married a man only two years older than me, but we still both ended up young widows anyway. I remember when Shaun died, when she came round to comfort me on the night it happened, one of the things she said was, "Oh I knew it'd happen to me, but not you, not so soon." Maybe the way Mum handled life after Dad's death shaped the way

I've been after losing Shaun: just carry on, go about your business and accept that a relationship's just not something that's going to feature in your life anymore. And since Mum's never suggested I look for anyone else, or asked if I'm interested in finding someone new, I guess that could be how she thinks I should live, too.

I don't want it to be like that, though.

"Mum, I want to tell you something. Something... well, it's nothing bad, but it could be life-changing."

Okay, maybe that was a bit dramatic. Still, as I've just said, given my circumstances this *is* a big deal. She stops thumbing through the TV guide and turns towards me. There's a look of distinct worry on her face.

"Is everything okay, love? There's nothing wrong with Jamie, is there?" Like any grandmother, Mum adores Jamie. Maybe even more than the average nan, because I guess Jamie and I are all she's got.

"She's fine, we're both fine, Mum," I say hurriedly. "It's not anything like that. It's just, well,"

I can see her waiting, eyebrows raised.

"I don't know if you've noticed, but I'm not wearing my wedding ring today. I've been leaving it off quite a few times recently. And the other day, when I was asked about my marital status, I said I was a Ms, not Mrs. I think... maybe it's time I looked for someone else."

She glances at my hand, before saying, "Well yes, I did notice it wasn't on the window sill with your watch when we did the washing up, but... are you sure, love? Jamie doesn't need a father, she's got everyone around her."

At the mention of her name, Jamie looks up. We tell her it's nothing and she goes back to watching her film. However, after that, I gesture with my eyes to Mum that we should continue our conversation in the kitchen. As soon as we're both out of Jamie's earshot, I say, "No, she doesn't need a father – and who said I'm looking for one?"

Well, I guess her attitude confirms what I feared. She isn't keen on the idea of me being with anyone else. Why, though? I said it was something important because hopefully it'll lead to some big changes in my life, the biggest I've had in years, but it's not exactly a bad thing, is it? A little bit of me hoped she'd be pleased that I was finally thinking about moving on.

I fill the kettle. This situation needs tea.

Mum sounds confused. "Well, if it's not that, what is it then?"

I flick the switch of the kettle on and get a couple of mugs out of the cupboard.

"Jamie does not need a new father. She never had the one she should have had, but she's been okay, more than okay."

I sigh and bite my lip.

"Strangely enough, she's asked about whether she'll get one because her friend's got one, so it seems my four year old daughter can handle it more than my own mother, but no. It's not about finding a father for Jamie."

I plonk a couple of teabags into the mugs, only for Mum to remove them and put them in her teapot.

"Mum, has it ever occurred to you that maybe, I would like to have someone? Jamie's the most important thing in my life, but it doesn't mean I can't want some happiness of my own. Obviously, if I could meet someone, there's no way they'll see her 'til I'm completely sure about them, and it goes without saying they're gone if they don't get on with her. But even then, I'm not looking for some kind of replacement dad. Of course I wish Shaun was still here, but there's no escaping the fact he's not. Look at me, Mum. I'm 32 and I've been a widow longer than I was married. Does this have to be the rest of my life?"

Mum fills the teapot and puts the lid on. She seems reluctant to answer.

"Well, I suppose if you put it like that. It's just... well, Shaun was perfect for you. Don't you worry that you'd never be able to find anyone like him again? And what if you were to lose him as well? I'd hate to see you go through that again, love. Maybe you should just stay as you are. You and Jamie get along just fine, don't you?"

"I don't want someone exactly like him, just someone who had all the great qualities he had. As for the idea of losing him – surely I can't be unlucky enough to have two men die on me, and if you just mean what if we broke up, then I think I've been alone for enough years to know I could do it again! Look Mum, obviously the best-case scenario would have been that I'd have had Shaun around for life – my life, Jamie's life – but it just didn't turn out that way. It's been six years now. I think I'm ready to think about having someone else in my life, but he's definitely not some kind of replacement for Shaun."

Passing me my tea, Mum's face is a bit surprised.

"He's?" she asks. "The way you're talking, sounds like you've already got someone. You're not just talking about the idea of a new man, are you? There's an actual person involved here." Her surprise turns again to concern. "How long has it been going on? Has Jamie seen him?"

Time to confess, I suppose. I don't tell her absolutely everything (especially not the hanging around bars hoping to see Rob when I'd told her I was watching a play or something), just that I'd met someone who'd set off a bit of a spark, and while nothing was ever going to happen with him, it made me think it could happen with someone else, one day. I certainly didn't tell her about pretending to lose my earring so I could give him my number. I think she'd have thought that was a bit pathetic and desperate. Her face softens while I'm talking.

"Well, it sounds like you've thought about it for a long time. I suppose as long as you don't bring anyone home who might be bad for Jamie... yes, I know, of course you wouldn't," she says, as she sees my mouth open to protest. "Other than that, if you think you're ready for it, then give it a go."

As we return to the living room to see what Jamie's up to, the framed photo of Shaun and I on our wedding day that Mum has in her hallway catches my eye. We didn't bother hiring a photographer, so the picture's at a slightly wonky angle. I think one of my uncles took it. We're on the steps of the registry office, I've got a bit of confetti in my hair and we're both laughing. I look so much younger – obviously, because it was over eight years ago, but it's not just physical age. I almost look like a different person. My eyes are sparkly and alive. I don't think I've looked like that in a long time. I know I've always maintained that Jamie and I are happy enough together, just us... but the sight of the laughing bride in the picture really makes me think.

I'm ready to laugh like that again, and if it can't be with Shaun, it will be with someone else.

13

"Arrgh! That really hurt, Mummy."

"You've just done a belly-flop, that's why. Next time, don't lean forward, hit the water feet first and you'll be fine.

I've brought Jamie for a Saturday morning bit of fun in the pool. Because she likes it, and doesn't get to go to Water Babes anymore now she's at school. That's all, no ulterior motives... although if I did get to see a certain lifeguard trainer, that would be a bonus.

He doesn't seem to be around today. Shame. Never mind, we still have a great hour splashing about in the water. Afterwards, over the chips and milkshake for her, coffee and garlic chicken baguette for me (part of the all-new adventurous me), I spot a flyer on the table.

It's advertising something new the leisure centre are offering. Birthday parties in the swimming pool. Jamie's only been going to school full time for a couple of weeks, but in that short time I've already learned that kids' birthday parties are a big deal these days. You can't just do a few sandwiches, make your own cake and play pass the parcel in the living room anymore. These days it seems no one has a party in their home; it's like there's a competition on to find the most unusual venue – and then there's party bags. When I went to parties when I was a kid, I'd be given a piece of the birthday cake wrapped in a serviette to take home. Now you have to give everyone a bag full of hyperactivity-inducing sweets, a balloon and at least three bits of plastic tat as well – bonus points if one of the bits of tat makes a noise that will annoy the hell of the kid's parents from the rest of the day.

Still, on the other hand, the idea of not having a load of hyper kids running round your house for an afternoon – and not having to clean up after them – sounds like a pretty good idea. Jamie's already been invited to one birthday party at a soft-play area, and there were dropped chicken nuggets and spilt drinks all over the place at the end of the two hours.

I study the flyer more closely. A pool would be an interesting venue for a party, and Jamie's birthday is coming up in the next couple of months. It's a flat fee for up to 30 children, so she'd be able to invite her whole class. I know her friend Ava-Grace from nursery is in the same class as her, but I don't know if she's made any new ones. This would certainly help. I wonder if she'd like it?

I start discussing the idea with her. She sounds keen, well she would I suppose. When you're her age, the idea of any kind of party sounds great. While we're finishing off our lunch, I hear a familiar voice behind me.

Oh crap. Why did I go and have that stupid garlic baguette? It was really nice, but I only chose it because I was so bloody determined to be different and not just have chips like I always do when I'm here. Now I can't talk to him because I'll be paranoid about my stinky breath.

I stuff the flyer into my bag and get up from my seat. "Come on love, time to go."

"But I haven't finished my milkshake," she complains.

"Fine, finish it in the car then, but we need to

go," I say, determined to get the hell out of there as quickly as I can before he sees me and I floor him with my garlic fumes.

Damn. Too late. He's seen me now.

He's been wandering round the tables in the café, stopping to talk to anyone who's got children with them. Presumably he's been given the job of trying to promote the parties.

Hmm, I think. If he's going to be there, especially in those shorts, I might just book one for my next birthday, never mind Jamie. Well, she seemed to like the idea of having a birthday party here. I think this might just settle it.

"Here again, Nikki. You're not stalking me, are you?" he says, laughing.

Oh no. Just smile, like that's not actually true. For God's sake, face, don't betray me by going purple or anything. I can feel a bit of a burn starting up in each of my cheeks. I don't even want to laugh in case it sounds really false and gives me away. In fact, after that sandwich, I don't really want to open my mouth at all. I give him a strange, closed-mouth smile and make a "Hmhm!" sound.

Great. Handled that well. He won't think you're at all crazy now.

He looks down at Jamie, who's sucking up the end of her drink noisily.

"And who's this little monkey?" he asks.

I pause for a second. Usually, I never hesitate about introducing Jamie as my daughter, but then I've never had to do this with anyone I was interested in before. Of course I'm not going to pretend she's a niece or something; that'd be a terrible thing to do to her, and it'd be really awkward if the day ever came when I had to tell him the truth.

I'm still nervous, though. His reaction to this could tell me a lot. If it makes him shy away and not even speak to me next time I'm here, then maybe he was interested but he's been put off. I'd be sad if that happened, but I guess it'd be better to know from the start if a single parent is a complete turn-off for him.

But on the other hand, if he carries on talking to me just the same, what could that mean? It's relatively unusual for someone my age to be widowed, and while I'm not the only single parent in the world, the fact I have a child might make him think I'm with someone. Oh, I give in. It's a bloody minefield. I'm just going to speak to him, let my breath put him off and just forget about him after today.

"This is my daughter, Jamie. Jamie, this is

Rob. He's one of the lifeguards here. Mummy found him a flat to live in when he came into where I work."

Rob's face doesn't indicate any disappointment, he just smiles again and offers me a flyer. I tell him I've already got one, but that we're definitely interested in making a booking.

"Really? Excellent. Doing these parties was kind of my idea, so I really want them to take off. Tell you what, ask for me when you call and I'll make sure you get any time you want. I'll even boot the old dears out if they clash with you," he says - and accompanies it with a wink.

Don't get excited, I tell myself. He's only being nice because he wants the party idea to be a success, not because he likes you. The only thing he's interested in getting into is his boss's good books. Still, it's an excuse to call him. I know I gave him my number last week, but since they didn't find my earring (on account of it never actually being lost) that turned out to be a waste of time.

"Sounds great," I answer. "Anyway, we were just going, but I'll be in touch when I've decided on a date. Her birthday's bang in the middle of the week, so she'd have to have the party on the weekend before or after."

I hope he heard that: *I'll* be in touch when *I've* decided, not *we*. No partner I have to discuss things with.

"Nice one. By the way, I did look for your earring, but nothing turned up. Might have been washed away in the drainage system. That does happen sometimes, sorry."

I assure him it's no problem (I feel a bit rotten now for making him look for something that wasn't there) and say goodbye. Just before we leave the cafe, I hear him speaking to the man at the counter.

"A white coffee, please and, actually, have you got any of those garlic chicken baguettes in today? Don't know why, I just fancy one..."

14

I look at my watch. I'm outside a three-bed semi, waiting for the owner. It's an appointment to measure up before I put the house on our rental list. He's a couple of minutes late, but nothing to get worried about.

The man arrives. He's about forty maybe, fair-haired and dressed a bit more smartly than last time I saw him. That time, I assume he'd been doing some decorating because he was in jeans and a T-shirt that had definitely seen a bit of painting action.

Today, as he gets out of his Range Rover, the jeans look designer and he's wearing an expensive-looking leather jacket. From what he said when he made the appointment, I gather he's got a few other properties that could come Crostons' way if I find a tenant for this one quickly.

Obviously, I'm professional and polite with everyone I deal with at work, even when they slam my shoulder into a display unit, but I think I'd better go into full-on schmooze mode for this one.

"Mr McDonagh. Lovely to see you again," I gush as we shake hands.

"It's alright, just call me Tony," he says. "Right, you get this house rented out for me, and it might be the start of a good little partnership."

We enter the house. I get my tape out and start recording each room's dimensions. His phone rings a couple of times. He leaves the room each time to take the calls.

The house has been completely refurbished, but it's got no furniture in it, so we go into the kitchen so I can put the contracts on the worktop for him to sign.

"That's lovely, Tony," I say once I've got the signature. "Right, we'll take over from here. You won't have to worry about anything. We can organise any minor repairs as you've authorised, so we'll only contact you in the case of any major issues."

"Sounds good to me," he says, putting his pen back into his inside pocket. "I've always dealt with the tenants myself, but to be honest it was becoming a real pain. They'd be calling up over the slightest thing." He adopts a whining voice, presumably imitating past tenants. "Can you change the lightbulb for me? There's nothing on the telly! Oooh, it's raining."

I smile. "Well, not sure I can do anything about the weather, but we'll take care of everything else. Right, I'll head back to the office and start letting my list of tenants know about this house, then!" I say breezily, extending my hand for him to shake as I leave.

As he shakes me hand, he looks as though he's about to speak, so I wait.

"There is one more thing, Nikki. I was wondering if you'd fancy having a drink with me sometime?"

Oh. I'm stunned... and a bit disappointed.

I know I should be glad of the attention, but I suppose I wanted the first man to ask me out since I've been interested in dating again to be Rob. However, that was before between the revelation that I'm a single parent and my killer breath, I went and blew it with him.

Maybe I should say yes. Tony McDonagh seems nice enough. Okay, he doesn't exactly set the room alight with his smile, but he's treated me a lot better than some of the professional landlords I've had to deal with. I guess my silence says enough for him.

"Look, it's okay, I didn't mean to embarrass you," he says, obviously a little embarrassed himself. "I could see you weren't married, but I guess that doesn't mean you haven't got someone... or you just don't want to know."

Nightmare. It's true, I don't really fancy him, but I hope I haven't just ruined the chance I had of getting a string of refurbished properties on Crostons' books. But what was I supposed to do, prostitute myself for a deal? I don't get paid enough for that.

It's not just the work implications that I feel bad about. I wouldn't have expected him to be react like that; he seemed almost upset. I'd have thought a man who owns seven houses would just shrug a rejection off and think there'll be plenty of other women who'd be interested, but he's obviously not like that.

"Erm, sorry. Look, I think you're really nice, but I have got someone I'm afraid."

He leaves, and I decide to give it a couple of minutes for him to drive off before I head back to the office. While I wait, I think about my reason for turning him down.

It's not a lie. I might not be in a relationship, but there is someone stopping me from being interested in anyone else. I feel like I haven't made any progress at all over the last few weeks. All I've done is swap one man I can't have for another.

Back at work, I type up the details of Mr McDonagh's property before emailing it out to any clients who are looking for three-bedroom houses. Once I've done that, I reckon I can let myself have five minutes for a coffee. While I sit with it at my desk, I pass time nosing through a few entertainment sites. You're not meant to, but I know for a fact most of the weekend staff spend at least half their time shopping, and last time Drake tickets went on sale, I know Karen did absolutely nothing for a whole morning trying to get Chelsea's birthday present sorted.

I'm never going to get anywhere with Rob, and I'm not interested in anyone else. Let's just have a few minutes laughing at cat videos and just get back to work.

"You have got to be kidding me," Laura groans, draining her glass. I pick up the bottle and give it a little wave. "Ooh go, on, just one more. I know I shouldn't, but whatever. Not like I've got anything on tomorrow. Being unemployed does have some benefits."

"You can go into work for me if you like," I say. "I'd better just have an orange."

As I open the fridge and get myself an orange juice, she comes back to the subject in hand.

"He's got seven houses. That's literally, let me see, SEVEN more than I've got, he wanted to take you on a date and you said no because you're still hung up on bloody Baywatch Rob with his shorts and his teenage entourage? Nikki Dunne, I'm starting to think you're beyond all hope."

"Yeah, I know Laura. I know Tony seemed like a nice man. Maybe if I'd never met Rob I'd have said yes," I say wistfully, "but when he asked me, all I could think of was that if I said yes to a date with him, it was pretty much accepting that nothing'll ever happen with Rob."

She laughs.

"And what if it never does? Hate to say it, Nik, but what if he likes really tall redheads or something else you just aren't? Or," she goes on, taking another gulp of her wine, "you never get up the courage to ever speak to him, and then one day you go to your OAP bouncy sesh and see he's the one wearing a ring?"

"I know, I know, it's stupid to turn someone else down when I don't know what's Rob's thinking... or if he's even thinking about me at all. I guess it's just, well it took me so long to start thinking about being with anyone after Shaun. Maybe I've just got it into my head that he came into my life for a reason."

"Oh please. He's a lifeguard at the local leisure centre, not some kind of angel from above," she says, rolling her eyes. "Forget about him. Or at least, okay, you can remember him as the one who tickled your fancy and got your blood pumping again, but you need to find someone who isn't just going to be a fantasy... starting with giving this Tony one a call telling him you've changed your mind."

I rinse my glass and put it on the drainer.

"Rob's not *just* a lifeguard, he's like, the head lifeguard if he's training up the new ones. And it wouldn't be fair to Tony to do that. Okay, I might have to accept that it's going nowhere with Rob, but that doesn't mean I want just anyone."

"Fine," she says. I can tell she thinks I'm doing the wrong thing. "Please yourself... and if you carry on being so picky, that's going to end up being your only option."

15

"Chelsea, I'm just off to see that two-bed terrace on Wick Street. Just take any calls and tell them I'll get back to them as soon as I can - remember, don't say specific times. See you in a bit."

After she did such a good job as an office dogsbody in her summer holidays, Jeanette was eventually able to find a proper role for Chelsea. She's doing her A levels now, but during the weekends she works in the Lettings department as my assistant. It's been great to have someone around to do some of the minor jobs, it's freed up loads of time for me, but I have had to warn her not to say things like, 'She'll ring you back in half an hour' only for me to have to deal with an irate customer because I got stuck in traffic.

"No problem," she says. "See you soon."

The appointment's fairly ordinary; a reasonably nice two-bedder. I'll have no problem finding someone for it. If only I could pair people up as easily as I can match them to properties, I think to myself on the drive back to the office.

Back at my desk, I have a look at the names on my notepad. I can't say Chelsea isn’t thorough: she's got their names, numbers (even though most of them would be on the system) and even what their call was about. Then I spot the one second from bottom.

'Rob Jones. Said he wanted to speak to you about it.'

She's listed his home number as the one to ring, so I pick it up and dial without giving it too much thought. I'm not at the leisure centre with wet hair and stinky breath now: this is a work thing. He'll have called because there'll be something wrong in his flat. Leaky roof or something.

"Hello?"

Oh, it's still nice to hear his voice though. Especially when he's off duty and I know I'm not getting the polite, customer-service, super-friendly lifeguard Rob, but the real person. I know some people would find his job a bit of a turn-on, but I'm more interested in the man underneath the T-shirt.

No, not like that. Okay, not *only* like that... anyway, I'd better reply before he hangs up.

"Hello Mr Jones, it's Nikki from Crostons returning your call."

There's a slight pause at the other end of the line. I wonder why, after all, he called me first. Doesn't he know what he wants to talk about?

"Nikki, you don't need to call me that. Thanks for getting back to me. Erm, I'm not actually calling about my flat."

He sounds strange, as though he's struggling for what to say next. He's never been like this when I've seen him before – although it's only been about five times.

"Well, look, this might seem a bit out of order, but..."

No way. He's not calling to ask me out, is he? I've never had a week like it - first Tony and then this! I never got approached by clients this often when I was in Sales. Hell, I've never been approached by two men in a week EVER. Maybe everyone can remember that yellow T-shirt.

I feel a bit sick, but in a good way. I wasn't just chasing after him for nothing: he's interested. It's all going to fall into...

"I was wondering if you'd be interested in booking a birthday party for your daughter if I gave you a 20% discount?"

I'm glad we're talking on the phone so he can't see my mouth drop open.

"It's just, erm, I'm struggling to get bookings and, well, you did seem interested. I'll be your personal host and make sure it's her dream party."

I'm not sure what to say. I actually did want to book a party, I was going to do it next time I went to the Aqua Therapy class. In fact, I'd also even been rolling a few ways to ask if he'd be at the party without it sounding too weird around my head.

But now, I half want to tell him to get stuffed. He's obviously not the least bit interested, he's just using me to get his idea off the ground. I'm not sure I want to sit through two hours of being with him now I know he couldn't care less about me.

I can't really tell him to get stuffed though, can I? Jamie's actually looking forward to the idea of the party, and he's just promised to pull out all the stops to make it great for her – at a discounted price as well. I'd be stupid to say no to that just because I can't have him.

"Sure, I will book the party. Can she have 5pm on the first Saturday in November?"

"Nikki, like I said, you can have any time you want. I'll shift things around to make it happen."

Hmm. If you're ringing me up like this, I doubt there's a lot to shift, I think, but I say nothing. I'm getting a good deal out of this. Financially, if nothing else.

"Excellent, I've booked you in now," he says cheerily. "I've already got your number from when you lost the earring. Oh yeah, I see you tracked another pair down. How'd you manage that? Didn't you say your mum got them from a little market when she was on holiday and they were one-offs?"

Once again, I'm glad we're on the phone, but this time it's so that he can't see me cringe. I've been wearing the 'lost' earrings today. I took them out and left them on my desk just before I went to that appointment. I was having one of those days when your ears get a bit sensitive. Obviously, I wasn't banking on Rob coming by and seeing them.

I mumble, "Well, erm, they're not exactly the same. They're like them, but not the same. I definitely lost the other one. Yeah, I did. Really."

Good work, Nikki. Excellent. If he wasn't onto you before, he will be now. It's sooo obvious you were lying with all that stuttering. Sinkholes are an estate agent's worst nightmare, but I think I'd welcome one right now.

"Anyway, thanks so much for this, Nikki. I'll make sure it's the best party ever. All her friends will want one too," he says. "I'll be in touch again to get details like exact numbers and what sort of food we can provide, but I think we're done for now."

We most certainly are, I think, holding the phone away from my ear and rolling my eyes. Over before it even began.

"Bye for now then. Maybe I'll see you when you come in for your next class? How is your shoulder, by the way. Getting any better?"

"Oh you know, it's improving. Still got a few things giving me a bit of pain though," I reply in a deadpan tone.

Things like lifeguards who get your hopes up over nothing.

"I'm sure Jamie's going to love the party. Thanks, Rob."

It was Jamie's birthday last Wednesday, and she had a lovely day. Alan and Christine collected her from school as usual, but then brought her round to my house when I'd finished work to shower her with presents. Mum joined us and we went out for dinner at the local pub, where they put a sparkler in her dessert and sang 'Happy Birthday' to her.

Hopefully, today's going to be even better. It's the weekend after and we've just arrived at the pool for her party. We've got there a bit earlier than the guests. Jamie's in her new costume (with a little pink net skirt and unicorns on it), paddling in the fake beach bit of the pool.

Rob's done exactly what he said he would: the place looks great. As it's outside of the time when the pool's open for public use, we've got it to ourselves. There's a series of tables around the poolside for parents to sit at, and a party area further along, where a table is already set with paper cups and plates. Presumably they'll bring the food out later.

Rob and one of his trainees bring through a

load of inflatable objects, held together by a net, and tip them into the pool. Then he comes over to me. He's wearing his usual T-shirt and those shorts. Oh well, just because nothing's ever going to happen, doesn't mean I can't enjoy the view.

"Well, I think we're all ready now, Nikki," he says. "They can have half an hour playing with the inflatables, then I'll put the wave machine on for a double session. Next, we'll do some group games in the water, and finally we'll do the food and the cake. Is that all okay?"

"Yeah, sounds brilliant," I say, trying not to look too excited to see him. While it might be okay to enjoy the sight of him in his uniform, it's just occurred to me that Alan and Christine are here. The girls at work just gave me a bit of a ribbing when they could see I was going all doe-eyed in front of Rob. I don't think Shaun's parents are likely to react in the same way. I'm really going to have to act as cool as I can around him.

I look down at my hand. While I've steadily become used to the absence of my wedding ring, I've still been slipping it back on whenever I'd go round to see my in-laws. I know it's stupid, but I just don't know how thcy'd takc thc idca of me wanting to move on. As it is, I'm not wearing it today. Hopefully they won't notice but if they do, I'll say something like I always take my jewellery off before coming swimming.

Laura appears, and after hugging Jamie and giving her a card with £10 in it, she sidles up to me and whispers, "Bloody hell, Nik. I know you said he was younger than you, but he's an embryo!"

I shake my head at her.

"Not that one, you div. That's one of the kids in his class. He's over there," I say, pointing him out.

Laura takes a good look at Rob. After all, she can look as much as she wants without it seeming suspicious. She's heard me talk about him for ages, but they don't know each other from Adam.

"You know what, Nik? I approve. Okay, you know I'm not really into dark hair and brown eyes, but he's pretty fit. Nice bum, definitely," she purrs as he turns around, oblivious to the fact that he's being watched.

I sigh.

"It really doesn't matter whether you approve or not now, though. He's not interested. He rang me up to arrange the party, nothing else.

I'm just going to forget about him. Anyway, I think these might be the first guests arriving," I tell her as I notice a couple of kids who look Jamie's age, holding wrapped presents, "so let's just get on with the party."

The party goes, go on, I'll use a dreadful pun... swimmingly. A lot of the kids, Jamie included, aren't confident on their own in the water yet, so some of the parents get into the pool to play with them and be on hand to grab them if they slip. When it's time for the kids to have their nuggets, chips and ice cream, I go to change along with the other parents.

I don't really know any of them. I've met Ava-Grace's mum a few times when our girls have had playdates together, and there's a boy in her class whose parents bought a house from Crostons last year so they recognised me, but other than that, they're all new to me.

When we're dressed and sitting at the parents' tables, we exchange polite small talk. One of the mums congratulates me on the party, saying she wouldn't have thought of a swimming pool as a venue herself.

"My Kane's not five 'til next June, but I think he might be having his party here," another mum says, "as long as I can have that Rob doing it."

I don’t really want to say anything in reply, which she interprets as disdain.

"Don’t you think he's fit? I know I wouldn't kick him out of bed," she says, "I'm thinking of jumping in and pretending to drown so he can give me the kiss of life!"

Just at that moment, Rob comes over to our table.

"Are you happy with how everything's gone, Nikki?" he asks.

I just about manage a smile.

"It's been brilliant, Rob, Jamie's had a fantastic time."

He asks to me to fill in a feedback form and he's about to leave, when Kane's mum pipes up.

"Actually... Rob. Could you give me one of those flyers you had before, the ones about swimming lessons? It's not my boy's birthday for a few months, but I think I want to start coming here a bit more often. I wouldn’t mind seeing if I can get really fit," she pauses, "like you."

Rob gives a terrified smile and says he'll go back to reception and get her a flyer. At least he didn't seem to enjoy her flattery.

I can feel myself getting flushed with annoyance, I'm really pissed off now. It's bad enough thinking I can't have Rob, without having to watch this other woman drooling over him and making no secret of it that she fancies him.

She watches him leave, before leaning in and saying, "I'm not that bothered about Kane learning to swim, I just want to have another chance to talk to him. I might ask what time he finishes. Kane's going to his dad's tonight."

"Wow," I say, hoping my nerves don't betray me and allow people to see what I'm really thinking, "I'd never have the confidence to ask a man out." I look around the pool area for Laura. "Hey, I'm going to go and see how the kids are getting on, but well, good luck with him, eh?"

I scuttle across to the kids' party table, where Laura is passing a big catering bottle of tomato sauce across the table. When I tell her about the conversation I've just had, we move to a corner.

"You've got to get in there first, then," she says. "Look at the state of her, she's rough as. There's no way he'd pick her over you. And just because he wants these parties to work, doesn't mean there's no way he could be interested in you. In fact, he probably called you because he likes you and wanted you to be impressed with him."

"Oh, I don't know Laura, I've never asked a man out in my life," I say with resignation.

"Okay then, leave it. But you can't complain if next time you come for your aqua class, he's covered in love bites from Little Miss Horny over there."

After all of the guests have gone, clutching party bags - I know what I said, but you can't not do them if everyone else does them. I'll get blacklisted by the mum's Mafia and Jamie'll probably never get invited to another party again 'til she's at uni - I start gathering up the presents to take them to my car.

Rob comes over and says, "Okay if I take this?", holding up the feedback form.

"Sure, no problem," I reply, turning round to peer at him over my armful of boxes. "Don't worry, I've given you a rave review. Anyway, I think you'll definitely be getting some bookings after this... and I think you're in there with Kane's mum," I add teasingly.

He looks around before almost whispering, "Oh, is she one of your friends or just someone you know because of Jamie?"

Once I've assured him that I've never met the woman before today, so she's certainly not someone I'd call a mate, he looks relieved.

"Jeez, Nikki, what was she like? She wasn't exactly subtle, was she?"

My turn to look relieved.

"So you're not interested then?"

He laughs.

"Hell, no. I think she'd eat me alive. I like girls who are more..."

He stops himself halfway through his sentence, before changing the subject.

"So, could Jamie's dad not make it?"

I'm not imagining it. He *is* glancing at my left hand. Come on Nikki, even if he's not interested, this is something you have to do. You have to get used to telling people you're available... or at least, not keep pretending you're still married.

I look up at him.

"No. My husband died five and a half years ago, before Jamie was born."

With those words, his face changes. He moves his hands halfway to his mouth, as if to cover it, then moves them back down again in a nervous, oh-no-I've-put-my-foot-in-it, manner.

"Oh God, Nikki, I'm so sorry. I shouldn't have..."

"Rob, don't be. It's okay. Life's got to go on, hasn't it?"

He gives me a last smile.

"Look, I'm glad Jamie enjoyed it. I'd love it if you could spread the word a bit. See you next week for your next Aqua Therapy session, eh?"

"Actually, I think I'm done now. Work let me out for eight weeks, and time's up."

In more ways than one. He actually looks a bit crestfallen.

"Oh, right. Guess I'll see you round, then."

16

Jamie's party, or as I refer to it mentally, the last time I saw Rob, was just over two weeks ago now. I'm fine with it. He was nice, okay, *really* nice, but it didn't happen. I guess I've got to learn from the experience and not dither about too much if I see someone I like again. I'll have to accept that, since I'm not a teenager anymore, people are more likely to assume I'm off the market. So, while that yellow T-shirt's an absolute last resort, I think in future I'm going to have to start being a bit more assertive and let men know I'm out there.

Just need to find someone I like the look of now. That's the hard part. That Tony wasn't my type at all, so I'm not too surprised I felt nothing for him. However, over the last couple of weeks I've been actively looking around for someone in every situation apart from work, whether it's doing the shopping, taking Jamie to play areas, even when I'm just driving around. But no-one really interests me the way Rob did.

I'm being stupid, I know. Just as it took Laura giving me a verbal shake and telling me I couldn't be hung up on Shaun forever, I think I need someone to tell me to forget about Rob. I mean, clinging onto the memory of a dead husband's fairly understandable, but I can't just close myself down again because of some bloke I only met about five times, and never even had anything resembling a relationship with.

For now though, I feel like shutting down is the safest option. I know I need to start putting myself out there and being a bit more pushy, but it's not really me. I feel like I've let things happen to me most of my life. Sure, they're good things, maybe I'd have had the guts to rebel against them otherwise, but all the same I married a man who pretty much told me to go on a date with him, and I only got my promotion at work because it was offered to me. If I'd had to compete against one of my colleagues, I think I'd probably have just rolled over and let them take it. Just like I let the first man I liked since Shaun slip away because I was too afraid to tell him how I felt.

I can keep looking around, but I'd be better off just going back to the way I was before. I'll concentrate on being Jamie's mum and making a success of the Lettings department. That's all I need. It's fine.

"Nik, it is most definitely not fine."

Laura plonks her glass on the table. We're at the one of the pubs we found when we were staking out Rob's neighbourhood. We actually came to quite like it in the end, so we've been back a couple of times even though we've established he never comes here.

It's nearly closing time and she's at that point where she'll probably start telling me I need a man again – which is actually preferable to the other thing she might do. Let's just say, as a singer, Laura's a brilliant makeup artist.

"Okay, you're right. But I'm just not seeing anyone I like the look of, and I'm not going to go out with just anyone for the sole reason of being able to say I got myself back out there."

Laura picks up the pint of cider she got just before they called Last Orders and takes a large gulp.

"Okay. Just promise me you're not holding out for Baywatch Rob."

I assure her I'm not. Good job she's a bit pissed, otherwise she'd probably see right through me.

"Fine. Mind you, I'm not sure why I'm so worried about your lack of love life," she goes on. "I haven't had anyone in ages. If I don't meet someone soon I'm in danger of healing over."

"Urrgh, I hate it when you say that," I say, wincing.

She takes another gulp of her drink.

"Come on, Nik, get that wine down you. They'll be throwing us out in a minute." Then, returning to the subject in hand, she says, "Whatever happened to you finding me one of those fit single blokes who come in looking for flats? Frankly, Nicola, I'm disappointed in you. You've let yourself down, you've let your school down..."

"Oh Laura," I say with some exasperation, "there aren't any fit blokes! I get loads of annoying students who can't get through a viewing without taking a bloody selfie, or I get middle aged couples wanting to rent off a house they've inherited. There was one fit man, one!"

I pause to take a sip of my drink.

"And yeah, fair enough, I was a lousy friend because I wanted him for myself. And couldn't even manage that."

Laura shakes her head.

"Look Nik, you know I'm not being serious about that. But I am when I say you really need to forget about Rob. There's a whole world of men out there – alright, I'm not sure exactly where 'cause I can't seem to get one either – but he wasn't that amazing."

Well, I don't agree with her on that, but I know she's right about everything else. I scan around the room, which is emptying out now that they've turned off the jukebox. I spot a poster tacked to the wall by the bar.

"Tell you what, Laura? Do you fancy doing this charity quiz night they've got on next week? You always get a few teams of men at those things. And at least we know anyone we'd meet there's got half a chance of not being a total div if they're willing to try answering a few questions..."

"Yeah, sounds alright. Let's do it. We'll batter them anyway."

We might, actually. Or at least, she will. She may not have a high-powered job, or any job come to that, but Laura's really smart. She tested her IQ once and she's like, genius level or something. And she watches loads of quiz shows. She's got to have picked something up from that, apart from that time she had a weird crush on Bradley Walsh.

"Do you think that's the approach we should take, though? They might be a bit put off by two hotshot girls knowing more than them. Maybe we should get a few wrong on purpose."

Laura gives me her 'Are you having a laugh?' stare.

"Nik, that is so not happening. If their fragile male egos can't handle it, well who'd want a saddo like that anyway? Not that I want to bring him up again, but you said that Rob didn't seem interested in that other kid's mum because she seemed a bit brainless."

Okay, I guess that was bit mean of me, describing Kane's mum like that when I've got no idea about her. I just didn't like the thought of anyone else being with him.

"Let's be our incredible selves, then if there's anyone good enough there, we'll be beating them off... haha!"

Oh dear. She's definitely a bit pissed. While she laughs at her own unintentional joke, I get my jacket on. Yeah, let's do the quiz night. I don't have to make finding a man some kind of mission that takes over my life, but I know closing myself off from the rest of world's no solution either.

17

“Okay Jamie, do threes now.”

Jamie pauses for a second before starting to chant her three times table. Despite doing her homework (homework? She’s only just five, seems a bit much to me, I feel like she’s growing up far too quickly) on the computer and having ‘peer massage’ at the end of each day (something I know I certainly never had at any stage of school), it seems there are some things that just don't change. She even recites with exactly the same rhythm as I did when I was her age.

With one ear listening to her, I listen to the radio as I'm driving. It's nice. I like being able to take her to school. Makes up for not being there at the end of the day. As I manoeuvre through the groups of mums standing in threes and fours in the playground, I wish I could be one of them - hanging around to chat and not having to go off to work.

On my way to work, I stop at the lights on the junction our pub's on. They've got a poster in the window, advertising the quiz night. Sod it, even if only a team from the local convent and the WI turn up, it'll be a bit of fun. All the same, I make a note to spend a bit of time this evening looking up a few things that might come up, like capital cities or US presidents. I know we said we wouldn't care if the men (and there *will* be some there, pub quizzes are a real blokey thing) were intimidated by us, but they certainly won't be if I can't get anything right.

After I've been at work for an hour or so, Jeanette asks to speak to me. I'm not nervous, things are actually going quite well in my department. We had a big influx of students around the start of the academic year, which helped let out pretty much all of the four bed terraces we had on the books, and I've had a steady stream of families of the workers from an engineering firm that recently relocated about ten miles away, so I don't think I should be in for a bollocking. If anything, if the only thing she can pull me up on is not getting enough new properties to let, things are going so well.

Jeanette has a cup of tea on the desk for me as I enter her office, and she immediately gestures for me to sit down. Hmm. This is either something good, or it's way beyond a bit of a pep talk and she's preparing me for the sack. I search through my memory for everyone I've dealt with recently. I haven't made some major, sacking-offence cockup I don't even know about and someone's complained straight to Jeanette or Head Office, have I?

"So, Nikki, you're approaching the six month review we said we'd have to consider the progress of the Lettings department and, I have to say, I think you've done an amazing job so far. You've really proved I made the right decision in choosing you."

"Wow, thanks, that's really nice to hear," I say, smirking like an idiot. I've never been good at taking compliments. "I like to think I've done my best."

Jeanette takes a sip of her drink and grimaces.

"Urrgh, that's like drinking muddy water. That kid we've got on work experience can't make tea to save his life.

I look down at my pale-brown mug of... well, I said tea, it might be coffee actually, I'm not sure now. Either way, I pretend to take a sip out of politeness and put it down again, where it'll stay for the rest of this meeting.

"Anyway," she continues, "you've done very well. So much so, in fact, that I've got a proposition for you. Crostons are looking to extend the Lettings service to a number of the smaller branches. Even some of our semi-rural areas will have people looking for rental properties sometimes – and I was wondering if you've be interested in me putting your name forward as a potential regional Lettings trainer, under the direct supervision of Head Office."

I don't reply. I'm too stunned. This is amazing. True, I knew things were going well, but it doesn't seem like more than a few weeks since Jeanette had me in her office telling me things had to improve - and I've improved them, but I wasn't expecting this. When I talked to Laura about the idea of being in the running for that Lettings Manager of the Quarter award I didn't really think I'd have a chance, but this is even better!

Hang on though, I think. There's a couple of words there that arc giving mc a bit of concern. 'Head Office' and 'regional'. Crostons'

Head Office is approximately 170 miles away. Jeanette has to go there about twice a year for some Branch Managers' conference and she always complains about what a nightmare of a journey it is and how she has to stay over in a hotel. I had to go there myself for a training course before I took on the Letting Manager post. Presumably if they want me to deliver that training, I'd have to be at Head Office too. How can I do that with Jamie?

Then I think, calm down, Nikki. Regional Trainer, Jeanette said. They're not going to want you to have to go and live near Head Office. There's still the 'regional' aspect, though. That's still a lot of space to cover. Am I going to be able to do this?

I guess she can work out what I'm thinking.

"I don't expect you to give me an answer straight away, so don't worry about that," she tells me, moving her mouse around to get some information up on her screen. "And anyway, you need to know what the position actually entails first. I'll email you the person specification they've given me, have a look and let me know."

I know I need to say something and not just sit swallowing air like a fish on a riverbank.

"It sounds amazing, Jeanette, and I'm so

flattered that you think I could do it, but..."

Her face becomes more serious.

"Nicola, I'm not just being nice to you here. If I didn't think you were up to it, I'd just tell Head Office you were still getting to grips with doing lettings on a local level and let one of the other branch managers recommend one of their staff. You've managed to get your own department up and running, more or less on your own, in only five months. I definitely think you're the right person to train up new staff members as Crostons expands the Lettings service."

I can feel my face has turned red by now. She continues talking, which is fine because I'm still thinking about the implications of this new job. Guess taking Jamie to school would have to go out of the window, for a start.

"You'd still be based here, and you'd still be in charge of Lettings. That won't change. The difference would be that you would have to travel across the region to other branches to deliver in-branch training to new members of staff, or when Crostons opens a new Lettings department. No relocation needed, just some extra travelling, but you will get expenses to cover some of that – and of course, there's an increase in salary."

"Well, that's a relief," I say, allowing myself to smile. "For a minute there, I thought you meant I'd have to go and live down in Uxbridge. If I don't have to take Jamie out of school or away from everything she knows, then I'd love to do it."

"There is one thing that might be difficult at first," she warns me. "You will have to undergo some further training before you can begin training staff yourself, and this time it will be a two-week programme at Head Office. I know you've got your daughter, and I'm sure it won't be easy, but unfortunately there's no way you can take the position without it. Do you have any relatives who could take care of her for that length of time?"

"I'll have to check that and let you know. I'm sure her grandparents would want to help me out, and I have got a good friend I could ask to do some of it if I'm really desperate."

Jeanette smiles.

"You do that. I don't want to see you losing out on this opportunity just because you're a single parent. You've worked for this, Nikki. You deserve it."

18

Laura and I are sitting at the best table we could get in the pub. We wanted to get a spot close enough to be able to hear the questions without having to shout for them to be repeated all the time, and not too far away from the bar, either.

"Right, between you covering films, popular culture, languages and literature, and me on everything else, we're going to smash this," Laura says with enthusiasm. I told you she loves a good quiz. If we do win this, it'll be 90% her and maybe 10% me if some questions about Shakespeare plays or reality TV come up.

Laura takes a gulp of her cider, which she's drinking 'to keep my head clear, I'll have a wine after we've won' and writes our team name, the one we always use when we do this, at the top of the pub's pre-printed score sheet: Quizzer Sisters.

I take a sip of my wine and look around the room.

"Hmm, hope we do win the quiz. It'll make it worth coming out, considering our other reason for coming here looks pretty pointless."

There's certainly no shortage of men in here, just none of them you'd be at all interested in. All too old, the types who look like they grow their own tomatoes and have definitely been married for years.

Suddenly, the relatively quiet bar gets a bit noisier, as a group of about six teenagers crowd around the bar and start ordering. I root around in my bag for my phone for a last-minute check on a few major capital cities before they impose the 'phones away' rule, but Laura nudges my arm.

"Nik! Don't look now," she says in a low, steady voice, "but have a look who's with that bunch of kids who've just come in. That's your Rob, isn't it? I'm sure it is."

I've got my back to the bar, so I can't turn and look immediately.

"I know I've only seen him once, but either that's him, or he's got a twin," she goes on. "Who else is going to be that tall and hanging around with a bunch of kids? Actually, if he has got a twin, even better! You can stop chasing after Rob and just..."

I decide it's probably safe to take a look. Trying to make it look as though I'm trying to see if there's much of a queue at the bar, I twist around.

Laura's right. It's Rob, surrounded by some of the trainee lifeguards I've seen at the pool before, and a couple I haven't. They've all been served by now and they're standing at the bar area, talking.

"Right, Nikki, this is it. No more messing around. Neither of you are at work, you're both adults and if you still want him, this is your chance to go for it."

I look at the group of teenagers he's still with.

"Oh, I'm not sure, he's with all those kids."

"Well, fine," Laura snaps, "but if you don't do anything tonight, don't moan to me about it again."

I know she's right. It's been nearly four months since I first clapped eyes on Rob, and he hasn't just been the man who made me think about wanting a relationship again; I really haven't met anyone who interests me in the same way since. Maybe he won't be interested, but now I'm finally able to have some sort of contact with him without it being work-related, I can't waste the opportunity.

But what am I going to do? Storm over and throw myself at his feet? Grab him in an embrace, give him a kiss you could unblock the sink with and declare my undying love?

"Tell you what I'll do. I'll go to the toilets, pretend to run into him, say hello and see if he says anything back."

It's a good job I wasn't around at the time of the Suffragettes. If I had been, women probably still wouldn't be able to vote because all I could manage was to shout, 'Cooo-eee!' at the king's horse. Still, it's better than doing nothing I suppose.

I don't actually need the toilet, so while I'm in there, I give my hair a quick tidy and refresh my lippy. Right, no more sitting around waiting for things to happen to me. For once in my life, I've got to go for it.

"Oh, hi, Rob!" I say, touching his forearm gently. "I didn't know you lived round here!"

He looks a little confused.

"Didn't you? You've been in my flat."

Fabulous. That gives things away a bit, doesn't it? Best option is he thinks I'm an idiot, worst case is he realises what I'm up to. In an effort to try to fix it, I gabble, "Oh, of course I know where you live. I meant I didn't know you drank in here. I've been here a few times. My friend just moved in to this area."

Neither Laura nor I live anywhere near enough for this to be considered our 'local', but he doesn't have to know that. He smiles.

"Well, I don't normally drink in here, to be honest. I've just brought my trainees out for a drink. They've all just passed their NPLQ, that's the certificate lifeguards have to get, so they're celebrating. They'll probably just have one with me before they go off into town. At least I'm close to home afterwards. Anyway, enough about that, hello again! Nice to see you. How's your little girl?"

We have a bit of polite conversation and I congratulate the students on passing their course before the landlord announces that the quiz is starting in five minutes, so I tell Rob I'd better go, saying I hope he has a good night if I don't see him again.

"Hey Rob, we're going to stay here for a bit and do the quiz. I had a teacher at school who used to do them for us at the end of term and they were a laugh," Nathan interrupts. "Do you want to be in the team or you staying with your girlfriend?"

"She's not my girlfriend," he retorts sharply, before looking at me, "Oh, I'm sorry, Nikki, what's he like? You talk to a woman and they think..."

I smile weakly.

"It's fine, Rob, don't worry. Anyway, I'd better go and join my mate," I say quietly, before adding, "Hey, there's only two of us, but you better get ready to lose!"

As I turn to find my seat, I can't really hear what Rob says quietly to Nathan, but I certainly hear the reply: "What? That is her, isn't it? The one from the kid's party? I can't believe you still haven't done anything about it. Whatever."

"Okay, so at the end of the third round, we have a tie between Quizzer Sisters and The Crafty Anglers". As he mentions our team names, the landlord points first to where Laura and I are sitting, then over to a group of about six men, whom I can totally believe spend their weekends sitting at the lake in the park with a plastic tub of maggots.

"We'll have a ten-minute break if anyone needs to get a refill, then we'll start the next round," he adds, before putting his microphone back down on the bar. "Phones are allowed during the break, but have to be switched off again when we resume. See you soon."

He goes behind the bar to start serving the people who have begun gathering, and one of the more irritating Christmas songs of recent years begins playing. Bit premature, considering it's not even December for a few more days.

Anyway, I'm not really bothered about that. In fact, I haven't paid much attention to any of what's gone on in the last half hour. All I've been able to think about is what I overheard Nathan saying. It sounds like Rob could be interested in me, and certainly as though I've come up in at least one conversation, but what if I'm wrong?

"Right, I'll get us another drink and then we can get psyched up to beat that bunch of old bores over there."

"You take this far too seriously," I laugh. "I

want to win as well, but it's only a daft quiz." Like I said, my mind's elsewhere.

She gives me a serious look.

"Nikki, when it comes to beating a team of men with three times as many members as us, it is *never* just a daft quiz. Come on, we have to do this – for women everywhere," she adds in an exaggerated tone, before saying, "Same again?"

She gets up to get the drinks, leaving me smiling at how odd it is that she refuses to take most things in life seriously, but is willing to fight to the death over general knowledge trivia.

Pretty quickly though, my thoughts return to Rob and whether or not I'm brave enough to do anything about what I heard. It's awkward. For a start, I wasn't meant to hear it, was I? I'll look like a right nosy cow if he thinks I was listening in on their conversation. Also, as I've said, I could have the wrong end of the stick completely. Nathan could have referred to me as Rob's 'girlfriend' because he thinks I'm a total minger and he jokes about the idea of finding me attractive. Okay, that'd make him a pretty horrible person, someone I wouldn't want to be with if he did that, but that could be what it means, couldn't it?

"Here we go," Laura says as she plonks our drinks on the table. She takes a gulp of hers, then says, "Oh well, if – and it will be a very big if – we don't win, at least you'll know you beat Rob's team. Hate to say it, but you might be better off without him. If he can only score 14 points in four rounds, he might be a bit dense."

"That's a bit unfair," I reply. "He's on his own with a bunch of kids. A group of teenagers are hardly going to be experts on politics or 1960s music. And he just might not be into quizzes."

"Okay, but we know what he is into now, don't we? Or more to the point, who?"

Laura, like any good friend, is taking what Nathan said as a positive thing.

"No more messing around now, girl. Soon as this is over, get over there and say something."

I frown and take another sip of my drink.

"I know I should, but I just don't think I can. Anyway, they're starting the next round now so can we just forget about it for a bit?"

If only it was that simple. I spend the second half of the quiz trying to sneak a look at Rob whenever I can. His team are certainly arguing a lot over their choice of answers, whereas we're the complete opposite: I think Laura's given up on me and is just writing the answers down straight away, without discussing it with me. I throw in the odd answer if it's something completely obvious, but I'm not really with it.

Eventually, the questions are finished and we get a last drink while we wait for the landlord to check the scores and announce the winner. While I'm waiting at the bar, Rob comes and stands next to me.

"Well, I'm guessing it's between you and the fishing blokes," he says. "I had no idea you were such a genius." He pauses. "Not that I thought you were stupid or anything, just..."

I giggle, probably a little too much, like a twelve year old.

"It's okay, Rob, I know what you mean," I interrupt, with an enthusiastic smile plastered across my face. If I'm not going to have the guts to say anything to him, I guess I've got to try to seem as bright and interested as I can if I want him to say anything to me. That's if he wasn't joking, of course.

"So," I ask, desperate for something to keep the conversation going, "your friend's wife, the lady who viewed the flat with you, would she be due to have the baby soon?"

"She's had it actually, two weeks ago. He was a bit early but he's okay. They called him Ethan, but they were tempted to go with Bob, you know, after my dummy," he says, laughing a little and raising a hand to get the server's attention. "I've been round to see him, he's ace. Tell you what though, I know they always say having a baby pretty much puts an end to your social life, but nobody thinks about the new dad's best mate, do they? Chris hasn't been able to come out in ages, so I've had no-one to drink with, unless you count that bunch of nutters over there," he adds, nodding towards the students. "They're alright, but... well, you know. Still, this place isn't too bad, I might pop in here again. At least there'll be one person I know."

I'm not sure what to say to that. Fair enough, Rob doesn't understand what it's like to be a parent and I can't expect him to remember my circumstances, but I wouldn't have cared if Shaun had gone out for a drink after Jamie was born – I'd have given anything to have had him there at all.

I avoid saying something like, 'I wouldn't know' because that'd kill the mood, but it seems he remembers, because he puts a hand on my arm and says, "Oh God, Nikki, I'm so sorry. I've done it again. It's just... you don't expect someone as young as you to be... you know."

Young. Okay, I can forgive him.

"Don't worry about it, Rob, honestly," I tell him.

At that point, the server asks him what he wants, so I return to my seat and tell Laura about our conversation.

"So, he's pleased to see you, thinks you're a genius and he was dropping hints about wanting to see you again. Nikki, you are not leaving without him. If you don't tell him, I will."

I'm about to tell her not to do anything daft and that I'll deal with it, when we're interrupted.

"Ladies and gentlemen, your attention please." The landlord's voice reverberates around the bar, the microphone's turned up a bit too high. He fiddles with it a bit before continuing.

"Okay everyone, after counting up the scores, we have the results. In third place with 47 points, it's The Green Bricks."

A small cheer goes up from a group on the other side of the room and everyone else gives a little ripple of applause. Then the same happens when The Crafty Anglers are announced as coming second. That means we've won. Nice one.

Laura comes up to the bar to collect the prize, a bottle each of red and white wine. Then, she seems to be whispering to the landlord. What's she up to?

She takes the microphone from him and blows on the top of it. I do *not* like the look of this. Oh bugger, she's going to make a complete show of me now, I can just feel it.

"Don't worry, I'm not going to make some weird acceptance speech. I just want to say one thing, if nobody minds."

Well actually, there is one person here who minds very much, so please just shut up, I think to myself. I feel as though I'm physically shrinking in my chair, hoping I might become small enough to hide behind my glass.

"See this fella over here?" she says, pointing to Rob, who looks pretty stunned. "I've never really met him before, but I know his name's Rob Jones and he's a lifeguard."

His students have a bit of a laugh and one of them gives him a gentle arm dig. After that, I can't even look. Not at him, not at Laura. I just fix my eyes on the floor and wish for it to open up.

"Now, I know this because my mate, Nikki, that's her over there, has fancied the pants off him for months now and doesn't know how to tell him."

On hearing my name, I look up to see quite a few people have turned to look in my direction. I swear I am never going to speak to Laura again after this. She's not finished yet, though.

"So, because I reckon he likes her as well but is as hopeless as she is at doing anything about it, I'm going to have to bang their heads together, metaphorically of course. So, I'm just going to say it: Rob, Nikki, just get on with it, will you?" she says, before finishing with, "Thank you and goodnight!" and handing the microphone back.

I don't even want to look at what he might be doing. I just want to get out of this pub, find a taxi and hide at home for until I have to come out in thirteen years' time for Jamie's 18th birthday. I wish the new job was in bloody Uxbridge now.

Laura can see I'm not happy.

"Look, sorry if I embarrassed you a bit, but you were going to go round in circles forever if I didn't do something," she says. "You won't be moaning when he comes over to talk to you, and I bet he will."

I glare at her. He hasn't exactly sprung out his seat to come and see me, considering how her little stunt was supposed to be the green light he was waiting for. She can see how embarrassed I am and realises her microphone antics might have been a mistake. Her tone softens.

"We don't ever have to come to this pub again. If nothing happens, you can just forget about it."

"Except I still have to talk to him about his flat!" I snap. "It'll be so embarrassing, him knowing I like him and you doing this. Thanks a lot, Laura. Let's just get out of here."

Laura stands her bag on the table and arranges one of the bottles in it.

"Fine, but let me just nip to the loo first," she says, before disappearing.

I tell her I'll go outside to try to find a cab. I stand up to put my jacket on and am about to leave, when Rob approaches me.

"Hi, Nikki."

Is that all he's going to say? Fair enough, I suppose, I've got no idea what to say either. We can't just stand here all night though.

"Rob, I'm really sorry about that. My mate, Laura, well she's..."

"Possibly right? Well, she is about me anyway," he says. "Look, it's out there now. I have been thinking about you since the party, but I just wasn't sure what you'd think of me, and there's the fact you go swimming, and I'd feel awkward discussing the flat if you knocked me back. So I just said nothing."

I have to laugh.

"Rob, I've been exactly the same," I tell him. "Well, what do we do now? Not right now, it's a bit late, but... I've already got your number, haven't I? Just haven't been able to use it. Shall we go for a drink sometime?"

He smiles nervously.

"Yeah, that sounds great. Or why don't we go for a meal, maybe? Do you fancy the Thai place on the high street? Tuesday, about 7?"

"No, not there." The Thai restaurant's only been there for the last six months. Before that it was Churritos. Rob knows I'm a widow, and I know it's time to move on, but it just wouldn't seem right to have my first date with someone new there.

"I'm just not that keen on Thai food, how

about the Greek place on Station Road instead?"

He agrees, then he waits until Laura comes out so I'm not alone before walking back to his flat.

"See?" she says on the ride home. "Was I right or was I right? If I hadn't done that, you and him were never going to get it together."

"Okay, you were right, it has worked," I admit, before the realisation of it all hits me.

"Oh my God, Laura. For the first time in ten years, I've got a date. Help!"

19

"There you go. You look fab, Nik."

"Do I really? Are you sure this dress is okay?"

"Definitely. Look, if he can fancy you in your work clothes or when you've got chlorine hair, one look at you all done up and he'll probably propose by the end of the night."

It's Tuesday night and Laura's doing my face for me. I thought it was a good idea to ask her to babysit, rather than my mum – or Christine. And of course, there's the added bonus of her being really good at doing makeup. I give myself a last look in the mirror. No more time to agonise, I've got to go with this... but actually, even though I do say so myself, I look pretty good.

Mind you, getting a bit more dressed up than usual hasn't been the biggest thing on my mind over the last few days. I've been really nervous about how this date is going to play out. It's been a whole decade since I've had to do anything like this: try to come up with interesting/intelligent/funny conversation, sell myself (not like that, you know what I mean) and generally try to seem like someone he'd like to see again – provided he's someone *I'd* like to see again. What if, after months of waiting and wondering, despite being really fit and seeming nice when I've spoken to him, he's got no sense of humour or he's one of those arrogant gits who does things like click his fingers at the restaurant staff?

Restaurant. Why on earth did I agree for our first date to involve going for a meal? I remember on my first date with Shaun at Churritos, I ordered a taco. I didn't want to pick it up because that'd look like bad manners, so I went at it with the cutlery. Shaun said, 'Don't be shy, pick it up' as he did the same with his burrito – but my taco was shattered by then and it was really awkward to try to scoop bits of broken shell up with my fork.

Even though it won't be Mexican this time, eating in front of anyone you don't know well's a bit of a minefield, isn't it? I'm sure we'll both do the obvious thing and avoid any garlic-heavy dishes, but it's so awkward trying to have a conversation while you're eating. I just hope I don't end up doing that daft 'pointing at your mouth while chewing furiously' before answering a question that he's just asked immediately after I've shoved a mouthful of food into my gob... and then there's drink. Should I or shouldn't I? I certainly had a few drinks on my last first date, but that was different. I was 22 then and had no responsibilities; rolling into work with a bit of a hangover wasn't considered a big deal – not that I did it often. Now I've got a proper job to do in the morning and (I know this makes me sound really old but it's true) I quite fancy just driving and being home in ten minutes, rather than waiting around for a taxi at the end of the night... and I will definitely be going home alone. I've no idea what people expect on a first date these days, but if Rob thinks sex is going to be a possibility, he's wrong. Not while Jamie's asleep in the next room, in fact it wouldn't be happening even if I didn't have her. Not yet. Not 'til I'm ready.

The other thing I've wondered about is what social experts would call 'dating etiquette', or to put it bluntly, who's supposed to pay? It's not the 1950s anymore, I'd always be happy to go halves – in fact, since technically I was the one who asked him for the date, according to the generally accepted rules, I should pay for the whole thing. Some people are still a bit weird about this though, and without wanting to be big-headed, I've seen his payslips, so I know he's doesn't make as much money as I do. Would he be offended if I offered to pay?

Oh well, there's no more time to think about it now.

"Right, Jamie, you be a good girl for Laura and go to bed without messing about," I say, kissing her on the forehead, then to Laura, "Give her a cup of milk and she can have *one* funsize. They're in the top cupboard on the right. Word of advice: don't let her talk you into reading her a Mr Crocodile story, she'll want you to do all the voices. See you later!"

"Sure, no problem, have a good time," Laura replies, giving Jamie a sideways smile that tells me as soon as I'm out of the door, they'll probably watch 'Frozen', sing along to all the songs and have about ten funsizes each. Oh well, can’t complain too much when I'm getting free babysitting. I take one last glance at myself in the hall mirror, then I leave for my first date in ten years.

When I get to the restaurant, which is called Athena, I don't go in. A quick look through the windows tells me he hasn't arrived yet. Since it's a Tuesday, even though it's the start of December it's really quiet and I'd stick out like a sore thumb in there, so I don't want to go in on my own. Instead, I hang around under an awning, hoping he won't be too long because it's pretty windy and my hair's already blown across my face and got stuck to my lippy a couple of times.

Luckily, he's not the fashionably-late type. He arrives after about five minutes and says he hopes I haven't been waiting too long. I have to laugh.

"Well, we've both waited around for about five months, what's five minutes?"

We're seated at a small table because there's only two of us. There's only two other couples there, but they've got a long table right down the middle which is set for about twenty, so maybe they've got an early office Christmas do in later. Still, even if it gets really noisy later on, we should be able to talk easily enough to get to know at least something about each other now.

The conversation's a bit stilted at first. I begin with the polite stuff, asking him how his day at work's been (Not too bad, the pool can go quiet this time of year, not so many people want to swim when it's dark and they're worried about getting a cold) and if he's all ready for Christmas (More or less, yeah. I don't go mad or anything), then we're asked if we'd like to order any drinks. Having decided to drive there in the end, I go for a tonic water and he gets a beer. I have to admit, when it's time to look at the menus, I'm glad of the distraction because I've run out of things to talk about. I suppose I could start discussing his flat, but that'd be ridiculous.

Okay. Let's look at this menu, then. I've never had Greek food before, this place has only been here since last year and the UK has never quite fallen in love with Greek food to the extent it has with Chinese and Indian. From what I can make out, most of the dishes are stews of various types, served with bread and rice. Not too bad. I don't mean that in terms of the food itself - most of it sounds delicious - I'm thinking of the potential embarrassment factor. Not much danger of sending a bit of rogue taco shell flying across the table this time.

Having said that, who wrote this menu – Alan Carr? A couple of the dishes have really dodgy-sounding names. I quite like the sound of the pork dish because I don't cook pork at home much, but there's no way I'm uttering the words, 'I'd like to have Afelea' in front of

Rob on our first date!

Rob notices my subdued giggle and says, "Are you laughing at the names? I'm not surprised. I've been here before and I'd recommend you try the Stifado but you might throw your drink in my face."

At that we both allow ourselves to relax and laugh, and from that point the evening gets much easier. I do indeed sample a forkful of Rob's Stifado, and offer him a taste of my Afelea, which he declines because he's had it here before.

"So, you come here often then?"

"Yeah. Well, now and again. Like I said, not had so many lads' nights since Chris went off the radar with the baby though. I know it sounds a bit stupid, but I kind of miss that."

"Tell me about it. I'm not lonely, but being a single parent means you can't just pop out for a meal on a whim. I can't remember my last night out that didn't have be planned ages in advance."

That's not strictly true. Shaun and I used to do it now and again. I mightn't be able to pinpoint which time we nipped out to Churritos or a pub was the very last time, but some nights we'd decide we couldn't be bothered cooking and just go out instead. I decide against saying anything about that, though. Tonight's about me and Rob – and moving on. I sort of change the subject, or at least shift it away from the idea of me being single.

"When you've got a kid, the only places you eat give you crayons while you're waiting," I continue, "and everything's breaded and shaped like a unicorn. It's been lovely to have some proper adult food this evening."

"Sounds alright, I like the odd nugget," he says, smiling. "I reckon me and your little Jamie would get on great. We could share a box of 20 and assorted dips on a Saturday night. I'm a barbecue man myself, is she a ketchup girl? Most kids are."

Whoa! What's going on here? We're only on a first date. If anything comes of this, it's still going to need to be a while before Rob gets to meet Jamie. What he's just said seems a bit...

He reaches across the table and lightly touches my hand.

"Oh look, Nikki, sorry. I don't want to come across all weird. I can see from your face that I've freaked you out a bit. I'm not trying to..."

He's struggling to express himself properly,

but he goes on to say, "All I meant by that was, I know some women would think a bloke isn't going to want to know if they've got a kid, like it's a problem or something. I'm just trying to say that it's not, not at all."

By this point we've finished eating, so the bill has been placed on our table. After I was wondering about it earlier, he picks it up and reaches for his wallet. When I get my purse out I just ask, "How much should I put in?"

He just says, "Oh, right, if you're sure," and hands me the bill so I can see for myself.

Having paid half each, we leave the restaurant. I ask how he's getting home and offer him a lift. He accepts, although it's only a short distance. I know my mum would go mad at the thought of me letting a man into my car on the first date, but Rob's far from a stranger: I know his address, his workplace and besides, during our conversation tonight he mentioned that lifeguards have to be police checked up to their eyeballs, so I'm not worried on that front.

While I'm driving, he throws in a real curveball.

"Ha, I remember when I first thought you might be thinking about me. It was the earring thing," he says, obviously feeling confident enough to say so now that the meal has gone well. "No-one ever bothers asking about earrings unless they're really expensive – and if they were, they wouldn't be wearing them to go swimming in. Anyway, we have a 'lost earring' board on the wall. We stick them there and people can see if theirs is on it."

Oh well, I suppose it doesn't matter. It's all out there now.

"Yeah, I know that was a bit tragic," I say as we turn into his road. "I just wasn't sure what to do... you know when I said it's been a while. Well, there's been no-one since Jamie's dad. I just never really thought it was the right time."

He says nothing, but I can sense the shock he must be feeling. Perhaps he's wondering if I'm just using him to get my confidence back or something.

"But I really like you, Rob. The fact I haven't been with anyone for so long, but I wanted to see you... that's got to tell you something."

"It's okay, Nikki, honestly," he says.

I pull up outside the shop his flat's above and turn off the engine. After the nervous start to the evening, I've been quite relaxed in his company all night, but I start to feel a little tense again. Going into his flat (if he were to invite me) is completely off the table; he knows I've got to get back to Jamie... but what about anything else? Do I wait for him to kiss me, or if he knows I'm the kind of woman who doesn't want a man to pay the bill for her, will he expect me to take the lead?

"Thanks, Nikki. It's been a great night. Erm, would you like to do it again sometime?"

I don't have to think about that for very long. If it wasn't for having to arrange babysitters, I'd be up for it again tomorrow. He's been sweet, funny, decent – and he's cool with me being a mum.

"Yes, Rob. I'd like that. Well, you've got my number now, and not just the Crostons' Lettings hotline, haha," I giggle nervously. "Give me a call and we'll work something out. Anyway, I guess I'd better get back. I know Laura owes me one after making a show of us in the pub last week, but I'd better not be too late."

He says, "Sure, I will," then I can actually feel his nerves. He's not shaking or fumbling, but it's like they're radiating from him. Or maybe that's just me, because I'm no better. After a few seconds, he turns his face towards me, leans in... and we kiss.

We allow ourselves a couple more before pulling away from each other. For a few seconds, we smile at each other nervously, before he says, "Okay, 'bye then. Call you soon."

He gets out of the car and I wait until I see the light come on in his flat before driving home.

I've done it. I've met someone new, and not just anyone: I got the one I wanted.

20

I try my best to look normal when I arrive at work the next day, but I should have known I wasn't going to be able to manage it; every time I sneaked a look at myself in the pull-down mirror on the drive to work, it was proving impossible to keep the smile from my face. Hell, Jamie even commented that I wasn't grumpy or yelling at her to get ready today.

Karen nudges Jen as I walk into the small staff area behind the showroom.

"Look at that face, Jen," she cackles. "I think someone got some last night. Didn't you, Nikki? Come on, we want the details."

I had mentioned yesterday to the other women at work that I had a date, and that I was looking forward to it. They were both really nice about it, appreciating it was more of a big deal for me than it might be for the average woman. Hasn't stopped them giving me a bit of ribbing about it though. I didn't tell them it was Rob, obviously. I know they've certainly commented on the attractiveness of some of their clients in the past, but neither of them have ever gone on a date with one – and not just 'cause they're both married. It's just not really something you're supposed to do.

I reach for my mug and flick the kettle on.

"No, he was a complete gentleman and everything was very civilised. But if you must know, he did offer me a taste of his Stifado," I reply, giggling. This may have been a big deal, but now I've done it - gone on the first date since Shaun with someone I really like - I can afford to laugh a little... and admittedly, there's a bit of all-girls-together banter going on here.

They laugh at the joke, but I can see in their eyes that they're pleased for me. Even if I never see Rob again, perhaps this'll stop them pitying me as the office sad case.

There are no viewings in the diary for this morning and Chelsea's only around at weekends, so I shut my office door and settle down to some paperwork.

I've been at it for about an hour when I hear my phone beeping in my bag. Hoping it's not the school saying Jamie's got that bug they're all passing round to each other in her class, I dig the phone out and look.

The text reads, 'Hi Nikki. Just wanted to say again, last nite was great. Are you free Saturday? Rob.'

I can forgive him the spelling of 'night', I suppose. Shaun used to laugh at me for being really anal about refusing to ever use text speak and insisting on correct punctuation in all my messages. Still, at least he didn't write 'gr8'. *That* could have been a deal-breaker.

While I'm texting Laura to see if she could babysit, it occurs to me that I'm still thinking of Shaun, even when I'm reading a text from Rob. I'll just have to deal with that, I suppose. Moving on is never going to mean forgetting him, at least that's what I said to him last night before I fell asleep. In one or two ways, they're actually a bit similar: both tall, both into their phones (being a phone salesman, Shaun always had the latest model and Rob's got something that looks more like it's from NASA than Apple) and so far, the same kind of sense of humour.

Having got a reply from Laura, I text him back to say I can be free on Saturday and ask what he's got in mind, while wondering what exactly I've had in mind, albeit subconsciously. Is it a bit weird that the first man I've dated since Shaun is more than a little similar to him, as if I went for a replacement? Or is that just having a type? And is it still alright for me to talk to Shaun in my head if I start seeing someone else?

I decide not to worry about it any further and get on with my work. Maybe I shouldn't overthink it, let's just see how a second date goes first... then my eyes skim across the diary on screen to what I've got on for next week.

The first of my two weeks in Uxbridge. Obviously, I hadn't forgotten about it – that'd be pretty much impossible, given all the planning and organisation between both sets of grandparents to have Jamie taken care of – but it had kind of slipped back in my mind a little in my excitement about last night's date. Flaming typical. I finally manage to get together with Rob right when I'll have to go away for a fortnight... that's a long time when you've just started seeing someone. He might forget or find someone else while I'm away. I'd already planned to dash home for the weekends to see Jamie, but if I'm spending time with her and doing the mum stuff I haven't been doing all week, then getting a sitter and going on a date is definitely out.

Oh well, I guess I can see this as a kind of test. If not being able to see him for two weeks does mean he forgets about me, then he wasn't worth the months of fussing over him anyway.

"Let me do it, Mummy! I want to turn the key," an excited Jamie giggles.

I give her the pound coin and she locks our clothes away before we walk through to the pool area. I know going swimming might seem a bit odd in December, but it's what she chose when I said she could pick anything she wanted for us to do together before I had to go away. She decided on swimming in the morning, then a film with hot chocolate and popcorn in the afternoon, so here we are.

I didn't worry about whether or not Rob would be here. It doesn't really matter now I can call him when I want, and I'll be seeing him again tonight. Still, it's an added bonus when the lifeguards change shifts at ten o'clock and he appears at the side of the pool. The best thing is, now I don't have to freeze up or worry about whether I've done my underarms (although I have, obviously). In fact, there's nothing at all to stop me talking to him now, as long as Jamie doesn't work out what's going on.

On seeing us, he comes over to where we are. Jamie's practising jumping off the edge and trying to land in her inflatable ring as I quickly try to slick my hair back, hoping it doesn't look too messy. Suddenly, my 'It doesn't matter if he sees me in my swimsuit with ratty hair' attitude feels like a bad move.

"Hello... Jamie, isn't it? I remember you had a party here last month," he says. "Are you having a nice time with your big sister?"

Oh please. I look up at him from where I'm up to my waist in water and give him a raised eyebrow... I guess we're doing this, then. Pretending not to know each other in front of her. Fair enough, I was the one who flipped when he talked about eating nuggets with her on our date. I know he's doing the right thing. It just feels a bit weird... deceitful, even.

"Oh Jamie, isn't Rob the lifeguard silly?" I say, before he has to go and have a word with a group of teenagers who are diving in head first. After he's done that, from the other side of the pool he mouths, 'See you later' at me when Jamie's not looking, then smiles.

Our date was an early one. Laura came round to mind Jamie again and I arrived at the pub, the one close to his flat where the infamous pub quiz was held, for half past five. We decided on a casual evening at a pub where we could chat and keep getting to know each other, so we both turned up in jeans and T-shirts - no, definitely not that yellow one. I've no plans to ask to see his bedroom. Not tonight... and anyway, I've technically seen it already.

It was nice. Most of our time in the pub was spent talking, a lot less nervously than on Tuesday night, about the usual things you talk about when you're trying to get to know someone: music, films, family. I find out he's into rock (okay, better than rap), martial arts-based action films (hmm, not great but not too surprising) and he's got two older sisters.

I remember saying, "Lucky you," when he told me that.

I've never liked being an only child. Besides the fact that people always assume you're a spoilt little madam (and I think that's the last thing you could say about me), there's the feeling of missing out on something most other kids took for granted. Sure, I had friends growing up, but I always wondered what it would be like to have that closer-than-close bond sisters are supposed to have... or a brother. An older one, who'd have looked after me, or a younger one that I could have looked after. When we did talk about kids, Shaun, who had his brother as his best man, and I always said we'd definitely have more than one. It's a shame Jamie's ended up being an only child as well.

Now we're sitting with our third drink (a freebie from the barman when he remembered who we were, which was a bit embarrassing, but we didn't turn it down) and it's only half past seven.

He stops fiddling with the beermat he's been holding and takes a deep breath.

"Erm, Nikki, I was wondering... would you like to come back to my flat for another? I know you can't stay out late, but maybe, you know..."

Okay. I didn't freeze at the pool this morning, but I do now. I'm definitely up for being alone with him for a while, but am I ready for it if 'maybe, you know' means what I think he means?

I know I'm being stupid. I'm moving on, and that'll eventually mean taking things further, if we are going to have any kind of relationship. We're two adults, we like each other, I know Jamie's being looked after; Laura even told me to, 'Fill your boots, Nik, I'll crash on the couch and give Jamie breakfast if you don't want to come back'. In short, there is absolutely nothing to stop me.

Except for me not being sure if I'm ready for it.

21

It's weird being back in Rob's flat. The last time I was here, it was bare except for basic furniture; now, after nearly six months of it being Rob's home, it's a bit different. He's got a 45- inch telly, a games console (no idea which one, I've never been into games), a couple of sport trophies on the shelf and, of course, Bob. He's standing in the corner with a pair of hand-weights rested on his head.

The place is quite tidy. I wonder if that's because he's a naturally tidy person, or just because he was planning to invite me round – and let's not forget the fact that I'm not just a date, I'm still his letting agent. He wouldn't want me on the phone to the landlord telling them the place was a mess.

He opens the fridge and offers me a choice of wine, lager or Coke. We still don't know each other well enough to assume anything. I like that he's not trying to force alcohol on me, not that I need a lot of forcing usually. After having a few glasses of wine in the pub, I kind of think that I'd be best off not drinking any more, so I don't end up doing anything I might regret tomorrow, but he might think I'm being a bit frosty or that I don't trust him if I do that. I end up going for a lager and tell myself that I'll only have the one. That way I should be fine.

"I'd show you round, but that's not really necessary, is it?" he laughs. "It's kind of weird to bring a girl home who's been in your flat before you have."

"Tell me about it," I agree. "It's weird for me to be a in flat that I measured up when it was a bare shell. Once I've found the tenant, there'd be no reason for me to come back to the property until after they've left... and since we've only been running the Lettings department for six months, no-one has yet, apart from that skanky family who caused the neighbours to complain and give me a knackered shoulder. Ew, that place was in a right mess when I had to go in and do the inventory after they'd gone."

He puts his can down and touches my shoulder. On our date the other night, when I told him about the shoulder injury I had and how it still hurts a little bit, he showed me some exercises that he said would help. He looked a bit silly in the middle of the restaurant, but he was right.

"Tell you what, would you like me to massage your shoulder a bit, Nikki? I'm not a proper physio but I do know how the muscle groups work, and how to relax them."

I'm not sure about this. Is he just trying it on, hoping once I've taken my top off (because I don't suppose you can do it with my top still on) we'll end up in bed?

"No thanks, Rob," I say hastily. "I can hardly feel it anymore, those exercises you showed me are doing the job."

"Okay, no problem," he says, picking his can up again. "Just thought it might help."

I feel a pang of annoyance with myself. I've finally got as far as coming to the home of this guy I've had a silly crush on for ages, I hope I haven't just blown it by offending him. I've got to let him know that I'm only saying no to the massage, not him. I take a step towards him, so we're within touching distance, look up (and there's a long way to look, he told me he's actually 6ft 3) say, "Maybe next time if it's not better by then, yeah?"

He understands. He gives me a smile and says, "Sure," before leaning in for a kiss. I reach up to put my arms round his shoulders and we continue to kiss for a few minutes before stumbling awkwardly over the couch, where we can have a proper smooch session with a bit more comfort and less of a height difference.

We're there for about half an hour, kissing, touching, discovering each other. The top does come off in the end, as does his, but my bra stays on. I'm excited, but at the same time strangely calm about being with him; it's almost as if, even though this is only our second date, he's someone I can feel completely at ease with.

I notice the time. Nearly quarter past nine. Not late for a Saturday night by most people's standards, and I know Laura offered to take care of Jamie if I wanted to stay out, but I've got a busy day tomorrow. I've got to pack, for both myself and Jamie, then take her round to Alan and Christine before driving to Uxbridge in the afternoon. I'd better go.

When I tell him this, Rob reacts exactly as I expected – with complete patience.

"No problem, Nikki. You go and get everything sorted." He picks up the empty cans from the coffee table and puts them in the bin. "I wish you weren't going to be away for two weeks. Can I call you while you're down there?"

"You better had," I say, fixing my top in the mirror. "I know, it's the worst timing ever... but, can we meet up when I come back? We're not just going to leave it here, are we?"

He looks amazed.

"Bloody hell, Nikki, no way," he says. "Come on, I know it's a pain, but two weeks is nothing. It'll fly by – well, actually it won't 'cause I'll be thinking about you, but you know what I mean. I'm certainly not giving up on you after waiting this long just because you've got a business trip. Besides, if I did, I think your mate'd come and beat me up," he adds, laughing.

I laugh too, mostly at the thought of Rob being scared of Laura, but also at how sweet he's being.

While we have one last hug before my cab arrives, he runs his fingers through my hair and says, "I waited too long for you to just give up at the first little thing, Nikki. I'll be here when you get back, and we can do things as fast or slow as you want."

22

It's been an interesting few days.

I arrived at the Premier Inn on Sunday evening, then the first part of the week has been spent being trained in the art of... well, training, along with five other Lettings managers from the other regions Crostons covers. I'm flattered to see that, while we haven't all swapped ages like a roomful of freshers, I think I might be the youngest of the group. This, along with my new younger man... it's a definite ego boost.

The company are paying for the accommodation, including an evening meal if we have it in the hotel restaurant, which we do, partly because none of us have got a clue where we are, but mostly because it saves spending our own money. On a couple of nights, the six of us have arranged to meet together and chew over the day's training as well as a meal to the value of no more than twenty pounds, but some nights we've done our own thing, or not met as a whole group. Tonight, I had a drink and dinner with Vicky from the West Midlands region before coming back to my room for the evening.

The highlight of every day has been my nightly Facetime with Jamie. She knows I have to do this, and I keep telling myself it's only ten days really, since I'll be popping back at the weekend, but I have missed her. It's a rotten time for a mum to be away from her little girl, what with this being her first year of school. Before I went, she was talking non-stop about all the things kids get excited about in the run-up to Christmas, and about being an angel in the school Nativity play... that's the worst thing of all, missing that. I know this promotion's really important and a great opportunity, but it hasn't come without its sacrifices.

Still, after I've switched off from my chat with her, I haven't had to feel down for long: there's been my other nightly highlight of a call from Rob. I always leave it for him to call me because I'm never sure what time his shift will finish, but I look forward to it almost as much as I do hearing from Jamie.

Oh, here it is now. My phone's buzzing. Yep, it's him. I slip under the duvet and get comfortable (doesn't matter, he can't see me) while I accept the call.

"Hi Nikki, how's today been?"

I know it's only been nineteen hours since I spoke to him (he had a late finish last night), but I still get all excited at the sound of his voice. It's like I'm seventeen again or something. I haven't felt like this, blushing and smiling at the prospect of talking to my - I'm going to say it - boyfriend, since when I was first seeing Shaun.

"Oh, you know, okay. Watched a few Powerpoints, took a lot of notes, had my chat to Jamie, and now... I'm talking to you."

"My day was alright. Better than yesterday anyway," he laughs.

I laugh as well. "Urrgh, anything'd be better than yesterday. Thank God it wasn't Water Babes so I wasn't there."

Yesterday was the Inter-Schools Gala day and... well, if I tell you that Rob ended up having to deal with what lifeguards refer to as a 'Brown Alert', I think you'll agree he won the

'Worst Day at the Office' award. That was why he ended up finishing so late. He said it took two showers and half a bottle of gel before he felt alright.

We talk a little more about what else we've been doing that day, before he asks, "Nikki, would there be any way we could have a bit of time together when you're back this weekend? Obviously, Jamie comes first, of course you want to be with her, but do you think we could manage just a quick drink or something? After she'd have gone to sleep anyway, so it wasn't taking any time away from her?"

I don't answer. I definitely want to see him, but if I haven't been there all week and if Jamie were to wake up in the night, even at ten o'clock, I'd want her to be comforted by me, not by Laura.

Then there's the other thing, which I'm ashamed to say I'm actually a little relieved that this trip away has bought me some time to think about. I'm still nervous about taking the last major step and actually sleeping with him. How is that ever going to work? He can't come round to my house while Jamie's there. I wouldn't want her to wander into my room in the morning and find him in the bed next to me, and while Laura's made the offer, it's unthinkable to desert my daughter so I can stay over at his place. Having to do it for work's made me feel guilty enough.

Aware I can't just say nothing, I eventually say, "I don't know, Rob. I want to see you, I really do, but as you say, I've got to think about Jamie. You do understand, don't you?"

He's silent on the other end of the line. Is he going to get fed up with me if I can't just drop everything to be with him? This is hard.

Actually, no, it's not hard at all. If me putting my daughter first's a problem, then it's game over... I just can't believe he'd do that, though.

I hear him take a long breath. What he says next could tell me a lot about where we're going – if we're going anywhere.

"I totally understand that, and I'll wait if I have to. Just wanted to see you, that's all."

"Thanks, Rob," I say quietly. He is being pretty amazing about this, maybe not every man would be the same. Then I have an idea.

"Look, what about this? I'm driving back as soon as the course finishes on Friday night. My in-laws are bringing her home and putting her to bed, so she'll be there and we can wake up together on Saturday morning... but then, how about if we came swimming again? Okay, it's not a proper date, but we would get a chance to see each other. Maybe, since she knows who you are, we could have a coffee together afterwards. Jamie doesn't have to know anything about us, she's seen us talk before so she won't question it. What do you think?"

"It's better than nothing. Sure," he replies. "You'll just have to have one of those garlic baguettes to make sure I don't get tempted to kiss you."

After we've said goodbye and hung up, I think about Rob: how great he's being about Jamie, how patient he's being with my nervousness about dating after such a long time... and, later that night, how I think I'm ready to sleep with him.

The drive back home on Friday night seems to take forever, but even though I'm absolutely shattered by the time I get there, it's worth it. Sure enough, Jamie was asleep when I looked in on her, but Christine must have reminded her that I'd be there in the morning when she put her to bed. I was woken up by the weird sensation of a hand thumping on my stomach.

"Mummy, you're back!" she squeals with

delight. "Hugs!"

I hold her so tightly, as if I want to try to make up for the weeks' worth of cuddles I've missed out on giving her, before letting her hop into bed with me so we can watch some cartoons together. Hmm. The only way I could ever have Rob here would be if I kicked him out at the crack of dawn – and it's only twenty past seven now.

Later on that morning, I suggest swimming, saying I knew how much she enjoyed it last week. Delighted, she immediately starts digging out her rubber ring and armbands from the cupboard under the stairs, while I just think about how I'm going to keep from throwing my arms around Rob and act as though he's just a friend.

When we get there, he's patrolling around the edge of the pool. He's got his back to me when I first spot him. That's a sight I've missed this week, definitely. When he turns to walk from the deep end, he sees me and starts walking a bit more quickly.

"Here again, Nikki. Hi Jamie," he says cheerfully.

Jamie frowns at him and says, "Her name's not Nikki, it's Mummy."

Rob and I risk smiling at each other. In a way, Jamie's right; for the last five years, that's all I've been... but even being with him for two minutes is making me realise I'm definitely ready to be Nikki again, too.

"Mummy's a special name only *you* can call me, love, but my friends, like Rob, call me Nikki," I tell her.

Jamie smiles. "If Rob's your friend and he works here, can I have another party here when I'm six?"

"Well, you'll have to ask your mum about that," he laughs, "but in the meantime, if she agrees, we can definitely have a milkshake together after you finish swimming, can't we... Nikki?"

I know this is something we'd worked out together over the phone beforehand, but he makes it sound so normal. I guess being a bit of a people person's part of his job, but it's more than that. He's so brilliant with her. I can't believe how lucky I am to have got together with him.

"No," she says firmly. "I don't want that."

Oh. Rob and I look at each other. This is weird, she's always seemed to like him. He takes a step away while I wonder what I'm going to say next. As I've always said, I'm the adult and she can't dictate every part of my life, but if she doesn't like him, then how can Rob and I really go anywhere as a couple?

"Don't be so rude, Jamie," I say sternly. "Rob's my friend and we're going to have a drink with him afterwards."

I'm not letting her stamp her feet and get what she wants right now when he's done nothing but be nice to her; after that, if she really hates him, I'll have to decide what to do next.

"No, I want Rob to come to our house for tea," she says. Auntie Laura comes round and plays with my dolls and gives me princess makeup. I want Rob to come and play with me, too."

Rob and I look at each other again. This time, he's got a look of total amazement on his face and I bet I'm the same. It might not be her complete blessing for our relationship, but I don't have to hide him from her at least.

23

"I wish I'd taken a picture of you having the tea party with her," I laugh. "It was so funny when you were crooking your little finger and everything."

I've just come down from checking that Jamie's asleep. There should be no danger whatsoever of her waking up, she'll be exhausted from all the playing she's done while Rob's been here. He was brilliant, allowing her to dress him up or beat him at Shopping List, and of course, taking part in a tea party with her Igglepiggle and Peppa Pig dolls. I don't think he was making a huge effort to impress me; I genuinely think he's a good man who's willing to get involved with her, not just see her as something he has to put up with in order to get close to me.

Now we know she definitely can't see us, we tangle up in each other on the couch and allow ourselves to kiss... which becomes a bit more than kissing. Unlike at his flat, we both stay fully clothed in case Jamie were to wake and come down, but I don't mind admitting I'd really like to take it further now.

After a few more minutes, during which I can feel he's definitely into it as well, he pulls away from me, saying he'd better go.

"You've got to be up for Uxbridge again tomorrow, haven't you, and I'm on early as well, so..."

I stand up, hold him close to me and kiss him slowly. All my life I've not exactly been pushed around, but I've had all the decisions made for me – often in a well-meaning way, like Jeanette giving me the promotion – but all the same, it sometimes feel like I don't even have control of my own life.

Meeting Rob has changed that. He made me want to go out and get him. Okay, it might have taken a bit of help from Laura, but I did it. And while I have to consider Jamie, of course I do, I think now it's time for me to do what I want some of the time as well.

"Rob, I don't want you to go. Stay here tonight - if you want to, that is."

He sighs.

"Nikki, you know I want to, but what about, you know...?"

I kiss him again. He wants it too. This is going to happen.

"It'll be fine," I tell him. "You said yourself you have to be out early, so she might still be asleep by the time you have to go, and if she does see you, we'll say we had a sleepover. She has them with her mates all the time."

"If you're sure, then," he says, smiling. "Yeah, I want to stay."

When we've reached my bedroom after tiptoeing stealthily past Jamie's, there is one more thing I have to bring up before we go any further.

"Rob, I wasn't sure when I was going to be ready for anything like this, so I haven't had the injections or gone on the Pill or anything," I say quietly, fetching a box of condoms out of the bedside drawer, "so are you okay with these?"

He gives me a cheeky smile.

"Nikki, I'm a lifeguard. If it's round and rubber, I'm all over it."

While I sit in my hotel room back in Uxbridge on Tuesday evening, waiting for my nightly Facetime with Jamie, I think about how amazing the last few days have been.

Saturday night. I'm not giving you all the details, but... wow. All I'm going to say is, it was worth waiting six years for the way he made me feel, and I don't just mean at the time. I never thought I'd ever feel comfortable falling asleep next to anyone ever again, but we just curled into each other and it felt perfect. It was the same in the morning: he had to go early, but we still made time for a few cuddles before he went.

Over breakfast with Jamie, I was glad I wasn't supposed to be in work that day. If the women there thought I had a big grin on my face the day after my first date with Rob, the one that just ended with a kiss, they wouldn't have stopped taking the mickey out of me 'til next weekend the way I was feeling on Sunday morning. I literally couldn't stop smiling. Even Jamie noticed, making me realise I probably shouldn't look quite so happy when I was going to have to leave her again in a few hours.

After I've finished my chat with Jamie, my mood changes to one of dejection. Sure, things are going really well with Rob, and it looks as though we should be able to get away with him coming round to my place on some nights in the future, but being away from Jamie's been tough. It was her Nativity play today and I wasn't there. I could have been if I'd just been in work as normal. Jeanette's actually really good about letting parents out to see their kids in plays and their first day at school.

I even asked her teacher if they could film it for me, but that's not allowed anymore. As it was, Jamie gave me a performance of 'Away in a Manger' in her grandparents' living room, wearing the costume my mum made from a sheet and a circle of cardboard. I managed not to cry while I watched, because I knew she could see me, but as soon as I'd logged off, I had a few minutes sobbing. I know it's not the end of the world, but I've been her mum and dad all her life: today's made me feel I'm not making much of a success of either.

I've calmed down a bit and I'm watching the soaps when my phone rings again. It's Rob, so I click the telly off and settle into a comfortable position, ready for a long chat. I tell him about missing Jamie's play and how much I can't wait to get back home – for a number of reasons, him being one of the biggest.

"Me too. Last weekend was, well, I can't wait to do it again. I got the impression Jamie'd be alright with me coming around again, so it doesn't really matter that you can't come to my place so much."

"Well, maybe I could bring her round one time during the day," I laugh. "I bet she'd beat the crap out of Bob."

"Ha, yeah, I'd better warn him," he says, and I hear him doing what I think is getting out of his car. He often sits in his car and calls me before going home after the end of his shift.

"Erm, Nikki. The other day, you know how you said your hotel room looked out onto a car park next to the restaurant?"

"Yes," I answer. God, he's got a good memory. I'd never have remembered that.

"Look out of your window then, so I can see if I'm in the right place."

No way! He's come to see me! I can't believe he's done something like this.

I pull the curtains apart quickly and open my window. It's pretty cold, what with it being ten days before Christmas, but I want to make my location as clear as possible. It takes me a few seconds to spot him, but there he is, phone still to his ear, standing by the sign that points to the restaurant. I wave frantically until he sees me.

"So, can I come in or what? It's freezing out here."

I tell him to put his phone away and I'll meet him at Reception. Thinking I'd be alone for the evening, I'd put on my pyjamas, so I quickly pull some clothes on and, of course, tidy my hair up.

As I skip excitedly down the stairs to find him, I realise this is more than just thinking we can have a night together with total freedom. I'm like a different person.

24

Rob and I have been together for a while now. We decided to keep things low-key for the first few weeks, and anyway, he wasn't around much over Christmas. His family live in some small town just outside Manchester, about an hour's drive away, so he went back to see them for a few days while the leisure centre was shut.

We were both pretty busy as soon as Big Ben stopped bonging: the leisure centre was filled with the 'New Year, new Me' brigade, all promising to do the gymming and swimming religiously every day before giving up on the 14th, and I found myself doing my first regional training sessions across a few different branches. I was bricking it, the first time I had to stand up and speak to a whole roomful of strangers, but with the aid of some prompt-cards and a lot of deep breathing, I think I did alright.

Anyway, we didn't get to see each other much. While that was a pain, it did mean we didn't have to address the idea of when we should tell Jamie about us, or how. He came round with presents for me and her the night before he went back to his folks for Christmas and she didn't suspect a thing.

I still haven't told Jamie that Rob is more than just my friend, but before I could even consider that, I wanted to tell Shaun's parents about him first, even before my own mother. After all, I could see it would have a much greater impact for them.

I decided this was best done after Christmas, to avoid any unpleasant atmosphere if they weren't happy about it. I was ready with my, 'I can see you're not happy, but I've got to be allowed to move on' speech all prepared in my head, along with assurances that Rob's wonderful with Jamie, but I needn't have worried in the end.

When I did tell Alan and Christine I'd met someone, and that I hoped it could become serious, they were as good as I could have expected them to be about it – better, in fact.

They said they knew I'd find someone else one day and as long as Jamie liked him and he treated her well, they'd accept it. Christine even gave me a hug and said it showed how important Shaun was that it'd been five years before I looked at anyone else.

"If you'd have run off with someone before Shaun was even cold, I wouldn't have been happy about that, but, well... life's got to go on for you, hasn't it?"

"Thanks, Christine. You know I'll always wish I could have spent my life with Shaun, but I'm glad you're okay with this."

My thoughts are interrupted by the phone on my desk buzzing. It's Jeanette on the internal line, asking me to come through to her office. Honestly, our rooms (she's got an office, I've got more of a glorified cupboard) are right next to each other. She could have probably just shouted and I've have got the message.

When I get there, about twelve steps later, there's no cup of tea on the desk and she's wearing a serious expression. This doesn't look good, but she can't have a problem with me spending less time working on my properties in this branch, not when she put me forward for the promotion in the first place.

"Sit down, Nicola," she begins gruffly.

Nicola. Okay, time to brace myself for a bollocking, then. She goes on.

"Now, you know I'm not one for engaging in office gossip, but to be honest, it's hard not to overhear at least some of it when Jennifer and Karen are yapping away instead of doing their ring-arounds. It's the biggest reason I saw you as the only one of the team I could trust to handle the Lettings department."

Saw? Could? Not liking these past tense verbs. Does she not feel that way about me anymore?

"My point is, Nicola, that I saw you as a professional. Someone who took the job seriously and didn't get involved in gossip, but..." she pauses, "I was extremely disappointed to find that today, you were the subject of it."

Oh no. I thought this might happen. Sure enough, when I told the other women that not only had Rob and I done the deed, but that we'd been an item for a few weeks, they were relentless in their good-natured teasing about my 'toyboy lifeguard'. Then, they joked that I was taking customer service a bit too far and did he get anything off his rent or just give me a large deposit?

"So, if I mention Mr Robert Jones, the tenant of 25a Whittaker Street, does that name mean anything to you?"

I tighten my lips and breathe out sharply through my nose. I don't know what to say.

Actually, yes I do. Laura's right. It's not as though he's a child or something. He's a grown adult who just happens to be a customer of the company. Jeanette and Crostons might not like it, but we're certainly not doing anything illegal. We're just two people who...

"Yes, he does mean something to me, Jeanette," I say, with anger in my voice. "No doubt you know this, since you seem to have been spying on me, but he's been my boyfriend for nearly two months. He's brilliant with my daughter, he's made me happier than I've been in years, and - and here's the key detail - he's twenty-nine years old! Okay, a bit younger than me, but there's nothing wrong with that! Look, I know I might have stepped over the line professionally, but I don't regret it and I'm not giving him up, because well," I pause, partly because I'm aware I've probably just lost my job, but also because I'm going to say how I feel about him publicly, "he does definitely mean something to me. There, I said it. Do what you want, Jeanette, I don't care. He's worth it."

Well, looks like my plans for the afternoon have just changed. I was supposed to be measuring up a new flat, but I'll probably be clearing my desk after that little outburst.

Jeanette is silent for a few seconds. Then she bursts out laughing.

"You're too easy to wind up, Nikki. I think it's great that you've got someone, I really do. I just couldn't resist having a bit of fun with you."

I can feel a red rash crawling up my chest. It's out there now, and even if Jeanette's okay about it, will Head Office view it in the same way?

"I am going to have to say one thing, though: it's not 100% professional to get into a relationship with a client, but from what I've heard, it began long after he'd finished having any face -to- face dealings with Crostons, didn't it?" she asks, looking pointedly at me.

"Oh yes, that's absolutely right," I say. "He rented the flat in July, but we didn't really get talking 'til we were both at a pub quiz at the end of November."

I don't think she needs to hear about the hanging around every pub in his area or Jamie's party. If I can keep her ignorant of those details, I should be alright - and if they haven't said anything already, I'd better warn Jen and Karen to keep quiet about Rob coming to my hotel room, paid for by the company, because I probably would be in a bit of a dodgy area there.

"So basically, as long as you didn't offer him anything inappropriate to get him to rent the property, or behave in an unprofessional way on Crostons' time, I haven't got a problem - and," she adds, seeming to understand my concerns about Head Office, "frankly, I don't think it's anyone else's business. You've just got to promise me one thing: if he ends up moving in with you, you'd better get that flat rented out again pronto! You finding yourself some sweet, handsome younger man who gets on with your child is all very well, but business is business, Nikki!" she laughs.

As I get up to go back to work, she says, "By the way, I was impressed by how you stood up for yourself just then. Showed some balls for a change. Didn't think you had it in you, to be honest," before narrowing her eyes and curling her lips, adding, "Twenty-nine? Ooh, get in there, girl. If I was twenty years younger..."

When I get back to my room, I consider what she's just said about me. I don't think I would have had it in me not so long ago. Until recently, I wouldn't have fought for what I wanted because I didn't want anything for myself much, but now...

"Hi, it's me. Can you come round tonight? I think it's about time we talked to Jamie."

25

"Hi, Ellie, and let's have a look at this gorgeous little man," I say, bending in to look at baby Ethan in his portable car seat. "You were just a bump when I last saw you!" then, to his mother, "Aww, he's perfect, and such a lovely big boy! Is he drinking up all his milk?"

"I've never seen anyone empty a bottle so quickly," Ellie replies. "He's a little chunk. Never mind baby rice, think I might have to order him a steak."

We're at a pub offering 'Free meals for Mum', so it's packed to the rafters and pretty noisy, but I don't care. This is the first time I've ever been taken out for Mother's Day. Don't get me wrong, between them the grandparents have always made sure it was marked for me, by buying a little gift for Jamie to give to me, or last year my mum showed her how to make sandwiches and treated me to lunch, insisting I had to sit in the front room and not enter the kitchen while they were working on it, but I've never had this experience. So yes, it is noisy, but I love the fact that Rob arranged it for us all.

His friends Chris and Ellie are here, because of course, it's her first Mother's Day as well. Ethan's five months old now, and needless to say, Jamie adores him. Ellie lets her give him a little cuddle, before placing him back in his baby seat for a nap.

While we wait for the food to arrive, Jamie goes for a play on the slides and climbing frame outside. We have a good view of her from our seats by the French doors, which have been left open today to allow everyone to enjoy the Spring sunshine - and probably to make the place feel less crowded.

"So, we get to meet you properly at last, Nikki," Chris says. "I know Ellie met you at the viewing, but I've been dying to meet his mystery woman." He takes a sip of his lager. "Honestly, he had it bad. After he'd signed for the flat but then you turned up at the leisure centre, he kept saying to me, 'Should I say something to her or what?' Then, when you had your little girl's party at the pool, he was like, 'I know she's not married, but I'll look like a right git if I try anything when she's told me'," he pauses, looking a little awkward and guessing he should choose his words carefully, "you know, about your husband. I didn't think he was ever going to get there."

Rob's clearly a bit embarrassed. "Alright, mate, no need for that, is there?" The look he gives me from across the table shows he's not too angry, though.

Ellie smiles at me.

"Tell me the truth, Nikki. Did you like him even when you were showing him round the flat? I remember thinking you looked all disappointed when I turned up and I thought, she likes him. Then, the look on your face when I said we weren't together..."

Doesn't look like there'd be a lot of point denying it.

"You got me. Hey Ellie, I put fresh lippy on and everything for that appointment. That's how serious it was!" I tell her, and we both laugh. Hopefully that'll have diffused the situation a little. Chris and Ellie seem lovely, and this is meant to be a celebration, so it's probably best I don't kill the mood by talking about how that was the first time I went without my wedding ring, or how I worried about betraying Shaun.

I'll admit, I do wonder what Shaun would think of Rob. I hope he'd approve: there's nothing for him to be unhappy about in the way he treats us. I have taken a couple of what feel like major steps recently, though. I've put away the picture of Shaun that I used to have on my bedside table, and I sometimes don't say Goodnight to him in my head before I go to sleep. It's not fair for Rob to have to see my husband inches away when he stays over, and if I want to let him into my heart, he hasn't got a chance if there's someone who can't love me back anymore taking up all the room in there.

Our meals are ready now, so I call Jamie in from the play area and we sit down. Right on cue, Ethan decides to wake up and start crying.

Ellie rolls her eyes. I remember that feeling; the countless meals eaten quickly and with one hand, while holding Jamie in the other and bouncing her on my knee. This is supposed to be a treat for Ellie, but she can already tell she's not going to be able to enjoy it much at all.

I decide to help her as soon as I've cut up

Jamie's pizza, but Rob's ahead of me. Ellie asks him to shift out of his booth seat, but he says, "You just stay there. You're supposed to be having the day off, remember? I've got him."

Ignoring her protests, he says, "You must have cold meals all the time. Won't kill me to have just one, and anyway I'll have him back asleep in no time." With that, he unhooks the harness, picks the baby up and stands at the edge of the booth, rocking up and down and soothing Ethan in a gentle voice.

I'm no biology expert, but I'm pretty sure it's impossible for your ovaries to actually melt... so why do I feel like that's happening to me right now?

After a few minutes, Ethan's calming down, but Rob's still rocking him when the server pops back to ask if everything's okay with our meals. We all nod and mumble agreement as best we can through full mouths (Laura reckons they definitely do that on purpose, wait 'til you're chewing then come and speak to you) and Jamie asks for some tomato sauce. When he returns with it, he looks at Rob in awe.

"Aww, that's so sweet. I know today is all about you amazing mums," he says enthusiastically, "but there's something about a dad with his baby..."

"Oh, no, I'm not this little man's dad, he is," Rob says, gesturing towards Chris.

The server's expression changes to one of undisguised disappointment. "Oh, sorry. Anyway, enjoy your meals everyone."

After a while, Chris takes the baby so that Rob can eat.

"Nice one, mate. It's good to have someone else take him off our hands for a bit," which he follows with, "and I think you're in there with that waiter. He definitely likes you."

"Yeah, well, he's out of luck. I'm well and truly taken," he says, winking at me and touching my thigh under the table.

We take our time, determined to make a proper afternoon of it. It's still sunny, so after eating we take our drinks out into the garden, where we can watch Jamie in the play area again. Ethan starts grizzling again, so this time I have him on my knee. It'll allow Ellie to remember what it feels like to have the use of her arms... and I don't mind admitting, I'm quite enjoying it. It seemed like Jamie grew up far too quickly, so I'm loving the chance to nuzzle into his soft, downy hair and get a lungful of the baby smell again.

Our peaceful chatting is disturbed by a loud wail from Jamie.

She's fallen off the climbing frame and, although she's about ten feet away, I can see a red gash on her knee. I've still got Ethan in my arms, so Rob springs up, picks her up and brings her over to me.

She's sobbing and the cut is quite deep for a playground accident, but it doesn't look like it'll need stitching, thank goodness. Ellie takes the baby from me and we walk Jamie back inside the pub. I can hear Rob talking to the server who was at our table before.

"No, don't worry, you don't need to get anyone. I can deal with it myself, mate. I'm a trained First Aider. Have you just got a kit I can use, please?"

A box of bandages and plasters is brought into the bar, and Rob does a really professional job of patching her knee up, all the time reassuring Jamie and telling her she's being a brave girl.

I decide it's probably best to take her home at this point. While Jamie and I say goodbye to Chris, Ellie and Ethan, Rob returns the First Aid kit to the bar.

"Wow," the server says, "your daughter's lucky to have such a smart dad."

Now the others have gone, I join him at the bar as he says, "Well, I'm not her father either. She's my partner's little girl."

The server replies, "Father, schmather. Whatever. What you just did, that's what a dad does. Take it from me, you may not be her father, but you're an amazing dad."

As we turn to leave, Rob seems to mutter something that sounds a bit like, 'Hmm, could've been' under his breath.

What on earth does that mean?

26

I remember when I was at uni, in first year, one of the modules we did was Creative Writing. We were asked to come up with a simile to describe ourselves. There was this girl in my class, a really annoying, overconfident girl who called herself Napalm because she thought it made her sound cool; no-one else did, we all called her by her name, Nadine. When it was our turn to reveal our ideas to the rest of the group, she described herself as being 'as bold as lightning', while I went with 'as calm as a paper boat floating on a lake on a windless day.'

As it was, the lecturer thought Nadine's simile showed (I've never forgotten how he critiqued her with a simile), "All the originality of a Xerox machine, this isn't Year 7", while he actually liked mine. Right now though, I think I'd describe myself as being like lightning as well.

Basically, I take the path of least resistance. Have done all my life. I didn't ask Rob what his muttered remark in the pub on Mother's Day meant, because I wasn't sure I'd be happy with what he might say and I thought, if things are going well, maybe I shouldn't stir up a potential problem. I just wrote it off as a random remark and we've just continued as we were, just seeing each other a few times a week and him staying over more often.

Have to admit, though, it's come back into my mind a little more recently. Now we seem to be getting a bit more serious. Sure, he always seems happy to spend time with Jamie, and the way he was with baby Ethan... well, I think that was one reason why Mother's Night was every bit as good as the day, but what if it's all a show? The dissent in his voice almost made it sound like he's not really into it, so if he's acting like a great father figure to please me, but it's not how he really feels...

Once again, I put it to the back of my mind, because I've arrived outside Jamie's school for her first Parents' Evening. Well, I say evening, it's actually 4.15. I've taken a shorter lunch to be able to fit this in.

When I get past the reception, I'm directed down a corridor to her classroom. This is actually the same primary school as I attended myself, nearly thirty years ago. I can't believe how small everything looks. I was the register monitor when I was in Year 6, and I used to feel like it was a marathon journey to get round every classroom (all six of them!) to put the registers on the teachers' desks every morning.

Looking through the glass panel of her classroom door, I can see Jamie's teacher, whom I swear is about twelve years old himself, talking to another parent. I look down at the tiny plastic chairs that have been lined up outside the room and notice that they all have little piles of exercise books on them, one of which belongs to Jamie. I suppose the idea must be that I can have a little look through them while I'm waiting, so I do.

Okay, I know every parent says this, but I think Jamie's pretty bright. She can write really well for a five-year-old, and I've always encouraged her to read. As I flick through her writing book, one page in particular jumps out at me.

It's a lesson from a couple of weeks ago, and the topic of the day was 'My Special People'. There's a photocopied worksheet glued into her book, featuring a picture of a tree, with oversized apples on it. Inside the apples, she's written, 'Mummy, Nanna, Nanny and Grandad', then, in the last apple, 'Rob'.

For a second I think, best not let Laura see this, she won't be too happy after all those free makeovers, but then I think more seriously about it. Obviously, Jamie sees Rob as an important person in her life, someone who comes to mind on a par with me and her grandparents.

There's no way around it. She really cares about him. Not just her; I really care about him, in fact I think I'm starting to really feel I love him and that we could have a real future, but if he's not 100% committed to accepting Jamie perhaps I need to put an end to it now. It'd hurt like hell, but I've dealt with worse.

"Hi, Jamie's mum?"

I follow the teacher into the classroom and am invited to sit down on another ridiculously small chair. He talks me through the work in the books and tells me that Jamie's a valuable member of the class who really seems to be coming out of her shell. That last bit surprises me, I'll admit. Sure, she's chattering away a lot more since starting school - being able to invite her whole class to her birthday party certainly did help her make a few new friends - but I never exactly thought of Jamie as ever being in any type of shell.

Having heard everything the teacher's got to tell me, I pick up Jamie's report sheet and am about to leave, when he says, "Can I just check, Mrs Dunne, that all of our emergency contacts for Jamie are up to date?" and shows me a piece of paper with mine and her grandparents' details on them.

"Yes, they're correct," I say, a little bemused. "She's only been at the school eight months. Don't worry, I'll definitely tell you if we move house."

The teacher looks a little embarrassed, as though he's said the wrong thing.

"Oh, I'm so sorry, it's just,"

I sigh inwardly. When you've been a widow since the age of twenty-seven, you get a lot of people feeling all awkward and apologetic when discussing your personal circumstances. However, he goes on to say, "Jamie's talked a lot about how she's got a daddy now, recently. Now, I know that you've told us, about... your late husband, I wasn't sure if you wanted your new partner added to the contacts list."

I'm stunned. I could tell him not to be so nosy and if I want anything changed I'll tell him, but that's not exactly my biggest concern right now. Jamie's never called Rob 'Daddy', at least certainly never in my hearing. I wonder if that's because of the chat we had, when I said you only ever get one, and that was Shaun?

Still, it shows how she feels about him, and the more I think about it, the more I understand. She wanted someone who'd play with her, teach her how to swim, read her stories. I know she always had me but, even at her young age, she felt the need for a dad to do those things for her.

If Rob Jones really is the man for the job, then I'm more than happy for him to be Jamie's dad. I've just got to know he wants it too.

The next day, he comes over in the evening. Once Jamie's gone to bed, we have to talk. I need to know how he feels.

We're slouched on the couch, arms round each other, watching telly. I give it about ten minutes before beginning with, "Did I tell you? Jamie's teacher said she's doing really well at school."

He starts rubbing his hand up and down my shoulder.

"I know, she's a little star. I pretty much don't read her stories to her now, she can do a lot of them herself," he says. "She's better than I was at that age, I'm sure."

"There was something else as well," I continue. "Apparently she's been telling her teachers she's got a new daddy. They showed me when she wrote in her writing book about the time you made her knee better and how you make sure nobody falls in the water. I did have to explain about the day she'd written that you live with a rubber man called Bob though," I laugh.

Right. He knows. His reaction to this is going to tell me everything I need to know about whether our relationship can really have a future or not.

His face doesn't seem to convey any surprise, in fact his reaction is quite the opposite. He leans his head back and lets out a quiet sigh.

"Okay, that's..." he stops. "Look, Nikki, there's something I have to tell you. Jamie's tried to call me 'Daddy' a few times. The first time was when she fell off the climbing frame on

Mother's Day, then the next was a couple of weeks after that. I was so flattered she felt that comfortable with me, but I had to ask her not to say it anymore."

"Why not?" I ask, although I reckon I know why. It's one thing to stick a plaster on a cut, especially when he's a trained First Aider, or to hold a baby for a few minutes... I guess the idea of really being a dad to a little girl who's never had one is too much for him.

"Well, because I didn't want to upset your in-laws," he says. "They've been nice enough to me when I've met them, and you've said they accept us being together, but I'd understand if they weren't happy about their son's child calling me 'Daddy'."

I look at him.

"But, if it wasn't for that, you'd...?"

"Nikki, I'd be more than happy for Jamie to call me 'Dad', if it's what she wants." He gives me a kiss on the forehead. "She's just the best little girl in the world. I love her, every bit as much as I love you."

"I love you, too, Rob, and hey, I'll speak to Alan and Christine about it. Explain that it's all come from Jamie. If I make it clear it's how she feels, that should make them a bit more willing to accept it."

Believe it or not, that's the first time we've said that to each other. I'm not sure why. We just seem to have almost not felt the need: it's like we both knew it, felt it, and didn't need to say it. We've just been happy to be with each other without needing any kind of reassurance... it's still wonderful to hear it though, and to know that Jamie feels she's got the dad she's always been missing.

There is one last thing I want to ask him, though, and right now, while we're establishing the terms for the future of this relationship, I think now's the time.

"Rob, can I ask you something? What exactly did Kayleigh do to you?"

27

He stands up and walks out to the kitchen, opening the fridge and taking out one of the bottles I keep in for weekends. Tonight's Tuesday.

"She didn't do anything to me," he says, sitting back down. Although he's making out it's nothing, his body language has completely changed. Whatever it was she did do, he doesn't want to talk about it - which makes me think there's all the more reason I should know about it. He sits down, but on the end of the couch, not relaxing into it.

"Look, I wouldn't bring it up, except if we're getting everything out in the open, saying how we feel and working out where things are for Jamie, then I think I should know everything about your past. You know everything there is to know about mine."

"She was just an ex. Everyone's got exes," he says.

"Yes, but not everyone has exes that cause them to move sixty miles away. That time we went for the meal with Chris and Ellie, when you were in the toilets they told me. They were being really nice about me, saying they were glad you'd met someone else after 'what that Kayleigh did to him'. Their words, not mine. You arrived round here with nowhere to live, staying in their spare room. Ellie told me how you just turned up one day at their door with your bags, asking to stay."

He takes another drink. "So I fancied a change of scene. Me and Chris have been mates forever, but he went to uni round here, and stayed when he met Ellie. I knew turning up at their house would be okay because he's my best mate, I knew he wouldn't say no."

There's definitely something he's not telling me, and at that moment, thinking of the other thing Rob said that day, I think I know what it is. I sit a little closer to him, in an attempt to make him understand this isn't some sort of inquisition; I just want to know everything about this man I've fallen in love with, and whom my daughter has been thinking of as a dad.

"Rob, tell me. When that lad behind the bar said you were a good dad, it sounded like you muttered, 'Could've been.' Is that what this is about? Have you got a child with this Kayleigh, and she's not letting you see it, so that's why you came to a new town? 'Cause if that's it, I'll try to help you, see if she can..."

He slams his empty bottle down. "Ha, no, it's definitely not that. Nikki, I can absolutely promise you I do not have any secret children I haven't told you about, anywhere."

He looks down at the floor, as I realise I've completely misunderstood.

As he knows I understand now, it's like I've opened a floodgate.

"Okay, we hadn't planned for it or anything, but when we found out, I was really happy about it," he pauses, "well, after the initial shock. I didn't do anything mad like drop down on one knee immediately, I didn't see that as being as important as, like, finding somewhere for us to live under the circumstances, but I promised her I'd do everything. I said I'd work extra hours to make enough money, or I'd give up my job to look after it if she didn't want to give hers up..."

I hold him, but I don't say anything. There's not really anything I can say to make this any better, just let him talk.

"Alright, I know it's the woman's choice in the end, she shouldn't have had to have it if she didn't want it, but why did she pretend? She agreed with me, said we could make a go of it, but she didn't mean it."

"So, did she..."

"Yeah," he says, spitting the words out while his eyes start glassing over, "she did. Said she was going off on a hen weekend for one of her mates. The whole time we were together I never once tried to tell her what do, but I did ask her if she should really be doing that, considering it was still early days. She just said she wouldn't drink and insisted she was going. I suppose should have known, but well, I didn't think she was like that at the time."

I'm still silent. I know what's it like to find out you're going to be a parent when you weren't planning it, so I can understand how this Kayleigh must have felt, but seeing Rob wiping the tears away and telling me how much it hurt him... well, he's all I can think about.

"Obviously, when I found out she'd got rid of it, that was it. I couldn't be with her anymore after that. It wasn't that simple though; where

I'm from, it's not that big a town, so I'd still see her around. It was too much for me, and in the end I thought the only way I'd ever really move on would be if I went somewhere new, where I didn't have to see her and be reminded of what went on between us. So, I packed my job in at the aqua centre and got on the train to see Chris."

"God, Rob. I don't know what to say."

He lets out a long breath.

"Well, you wanted to know. That's why I'm here. Not exactly over it, but until you brought it up, I was alright.

I wince and say, "I'm sorry, I just wanted to..."

"It's okay, Nikki," he says. "While it was a horrible thing, I guess I'd never have met you and Jamie without it. Meeting you has really helped me move on with my life, but I guess every now and then it still hurts."

28

"What do you think of it, then?"

Laura takes a large gulp of the wine I've just poured from a bottle we're sharing.

"Mmm, not the best, but you're not going to get anything amazing for £6.99 I suppose."

I shake my head. "Not the wine... Rob. What about him?"

We're sitting in a bar, despite it only being 2 o'clock on a Saturday. It was Laura's birthday yesterday, so Rob's minding Jamie (or she him, I'm not sure which) while I've taken her out for a bit of shopping and lunch. It was even his suggestion that I get the train into town so we could have a few drinks. Maybe he feels a bit bad for taking me away from her since we've been together.

"If you want me to completely honest, I think his reaction was totally normal," she says. "True, it's the woman's choice at the end of the day, but it doesn't mean he's not allowed to have any feelings. The ex might have had the right to decide not to keep it, but no, I don't think she should have done it without talking about it with him. I mean, he doesn't exactly seem the type to try to stop her."

I swallow a mouthful of my drink (mmm, she's not kidding, I've definitely had better, too sweet) and say, "Well, yes, that's how I feel about it too, but what I'm wondering is, do you think he's just with me to get over her?"

"What would you say if he asked you if you're only with him to get over Shaun? I don't think it's anything sinister at all. If you're thinking he's really only interested in you because it gives him the chance to play dad he was denied, I don't agree with you. Whenever I see you together, sure, he loves Jamie, but he loves you too."

I end up agreeing with her, but deep down, I wonder if that is what's at the basis of his interest in me. However, after another glass of the wine (tastes a bit better if you keep drinking it), I feel a bit more relaxed about it:

no matter what his reasons are, he's great with Jamie and we're happy together overall. I need to stop overanalysing things.

We change the subject, get another bottle and, because it's a rare thing for us to be out drinking in the afternoon, treat ourselves to a couple of this weird cocktail they've got on promotion... and two hours disappear in what feels like ten minutes. While we've been there, various people have come and gone. Laura spots two men come in, get drinks but stay standing by the bar.

"What do you think of him over there, with the sandy hair and the green shirt? Wouldn't mind a bit of that," she says quietly.

I look over at the man, who's facing in our direction and standing talking to another man, whose back is towards us.

"Not my type, not that it matters. Definitely yours though. Would you like me to see if I can make an announcement, like you did for me?"

"Worked, didn't it?" she grins. "No, I'll just flash my megawatt smile and he'll come running. Damn this power I have over men," she laughs.

Actually, she jokes about it, but after a while

he does come over and ask if we'd like another drink. The way we're both giggling, I think we've probably had enough, so I accept a Diet Coke but Laura lets him buy her a cider. Once I've made it clear that I'm not available for being paired off with his friend, we invite them to sit with us. Well, I feel a bit obligated. Not to the blokes, to Laura. It might have embarrassed the hell out of me, but she was responsible for Rob and I getting together, so if she needs a wing woman to chat this guy up, it's the least I can do to help.

Laura's man brings the drinks to the table, then his mate turns and walks towards us. His face changes when he sees me.

"Hello," he says, cautiously, "It is you, Nikki, isn't it? How long has it been since I saw you?"

"About six years, I'd say, Kieran," I reply flatly.

He used to work with Shaun. I remember they got on alright, but they were never what you'd call great friends. I'm pretty sure the last time I saw him was the funeral. Still, that's not important right now. Maybe having someone I've met a couple of times before to talk to will make this easier.

Kieran asks how life's been treating me, so I tell him about Jamie and show him some photos of her, as well as mentioning that I've found someone else, for two reasons. First, there's nothing to be ashamed of; after six years it's not too weird to think that I might have moved on, and secondly, I want to make sure he's completely got the message that I'm only doing this to keep Laura company.

"In fact, talking of which, look, here he is now," I say with relief as I spot him outside the bar, waving through the window. As well as taking care of Jamie, he even said he'd come and collect us so we didn't have to get cabs back... I know, and I'm wasting time wondering about whether he's The One or not. I need to wake up and realise how lucky I am, don't I?

I'm not really happy about leaving a half-cut Laura with two blokes I don't really know, even if it is five o'clock and still light, so I persuade her to come with us. I wish the two men a polite goodbye and come out to the car, while Laura swaps numbers with her man.

"Jamie and I have had a fun time," Rob tells us as we drive home. "We built a Lego city, went to the park and had pizza for lunch before I dropped her off at your mum's for a special Nanna sleepover. Have you had a good time, girls?"

"Yeah," I reply, "but I think I just want to fall

asleep now." Good job we planned ahead for the idea of the sleepover in case Jamie saw me getting a bit merry because frankly, I feel merry as a newt.

I'm not so drunk I can't think straight, though. While Rob's driving us round to Laura's flat, I look across at him. In a strange way, I'm glad I know about the circumstances that brought him into my life and, while I wish he'd never had to go through that pain, I'm just happy Jamie and I have got him, and that hopefully, being with us has helped him move on.

The way he has for me. Only a year ago, I may not have been lonely, but I was definitely alone. I wasn't miserable... but I wasn't happy. I just got carried along by life, just doing what I was told and not thinking about what I wanted. Meeting Rob has changed everything: like that time Jeanette noticed a difference in me at work. I don't hide away from being alive anymore.

Now, I feel ready to take the biggest step in my life, make the biggest decision I've probably ever made. I've been thinking about it all afternoon, and especially after what Laura said, I know it's the right time. I'm going to ask him to move in with us.

Not tonight, though. It's probably best that I wait 'til tomorrow, when I've sobered up. Then we can start making arrangements for him to leave his flat. Jamie's going to be delighted when we tell her.

Anyway, that's tomorrow. I ask Laura if she's planning to call Jim, the man she just met in the pub.

"Yeah, definitely. He was alright to talk to, I think we could get on. I won't do it 'til Monday, though. Think I need to sober up first. Hey, that Kieran was a cheeky bugger, wasn't he? While you were getting in the car, he said Rob looked like he'd been cloned from Shaun."

I turn to where she's sitting in the back and glare at her, but, probably because she's a bit drunk, she doesn't stop.

"He did! He said you could only have got someone more like him if you'd gone after his brother," then, seemingly realising what she's said, "Oh God, sorry. I'll shut up now."

There is total silence for the few roads until we drop her off. I get out and make sure she can get her key into her lock without any problems, then I get back into the car.

"Rob..." I begin.

"Don't call me that", he hisses. "I bet in your head, you've been calling me Shaun 2.0 all along."

29

"Look, Rob. I don't know why he said that," I say, once we've closed the front door behind us. "You've seen photos of Shaun. Apart from the height thing, I wouldn't say you look like him at all. So I like tall men – what can I do about that?"

I know when we first got together, I had a bit of a worry about this. I thought Rob did have some similarities to Shaun but, to be honest, I wrote it off in my head as just them both being my type of man.

I put the kettle on and ask him if he wants a coffee. I may be decaf usually, but I've started keeping some proper full-strength rocket fuel in for him when he's on an early shift, and I think I need a cup of that right now. I ask him if he wants a coffee or a beer.

"You sort yourself out, I'm going home. You'll be alright on your own."

We were supposed to be spending a cosy evening together, but it looks like that's changed. Along with my plans for what I wanted to discuss with him in the morning.

"No, Rob, don't leave it like this. Can we just talk about it?"

"Not while you're drunk," he says curtly.

"I'm not that drunk," I retort. "Trust me, Rob, I'm sobering up by the minute. I just want to know why you're so angry about something which, well, it's not even a thing."

He picks his keys up from the table and turns to go, so I try one last time. "Please? While Jamie's not here?"

He drops his overnight bag by the doorway (hmm, not bringing it back into the living room) and comes back into the kitchen. I offer him a drink again, which he declines; he obviously wants to be able to drive away at the end of this.

"Alright, maybe you're a bit like Shaun in one or two ways. He was tall, you arc. Hc had brown hair, so do you. Wouldn't it be stranger that I fancied you if he'd been little and blond?"

He still isn't looking at me.

"It's not that so much, Nikki," he says, sounding as though he's speaking through clenched teeth. "If I was one of a few boyfriends you'd had, and I happened to be a bit like your husband, I could handle that. It's that fact that you didn't have anyone for five years after he died. I know you wouldn't go off with someone new immediately after, but five years. That's a long time. What were you waiting for, a weird copy of Shaun to come along?"

"It's not like that at all, Rob," I tell him. "I just... didn't even think about why I wasn't with someone until I met you. I had to make sure I was being a good mum to Jamie first, I didn't think it was necessary to go looking for someone else. Then that day, when you came into my office," my voice starts to wobble a little, "it’s hard to explain, but that was the first time I'd thought about wanting to be with someone since Shaun. To be honest, I can't see why you're viewing this as a bad thing. How is it wrong that I didn't just jump into bed with every bloke I ever met, but waited for you because I thought you were special?"

"Because the reason you thought I was special was because I reminded you of him!" he snaps. "Do you know what, Nikki? This last year, being with you, getting to know Jamie, it's been brilliant. Best year of my life, but I'm starting to feel like you're only with me because I'm a substitute for someone you can't have. Oh well, guess me coming along saved you from resorting to getting one of those blow-up boyfriends from Ebay and calling him..."

I whirl round angrily.

"And what about me?" I shout. "Me and Jamie? Is she just the replacement for the child you didn't have with Kayleigh?"

I laugh, shaking my head. "Makes sense now. All that stuff about sitting eating nuggets with her on our first date. Saying you were cool with me being a single parent – I bet you were! It's the only thing you're really interested in me for, isn't it?"

He looks angry now. His voice takes on an offended tone.

"Nikki, what the hell are you trying to say? I love Jamie, I'm not..."

"No, I know you're not dodgy, I'm not saying that. But answer me this: is the fact you get to play daddy with her the reason we're doing this?"

He walks towards the door and picks up his bag. With the front door open, he turns and says, "There's no answer I can give you that'll be okay, is there? If I say no, I'm not interested in being a dad to her, then I'm a heartless bastard, but if I say I love her and want to be there for her, you'll say that's all I'm interested in. I can't win. See you, Nikki."

I don't try to stop him going or ask him to stay, doesn't look like there'd be any point.

For the rest of the evening, I keep glancing at my phone, but he doesn't get in touch. I shouldn't be surprised; I don't know what I'd say to him right now, either. All I can feel is the realisation, like a weight sitting on my chest, of knowing I've only ever loved two men in my life - and now I've gone and lost both of them.

"Rob's just busy, love. Maybe he's had to go away for work, remember like I had to before Christmas and now?"

This is why I should have never got involved

with anyone again. Why I stayed on my own for so long after Shaun. I'll just have to deal with how I'm feeling, but now Jamie's got attached to him, and eventually, when I have to tell her that she's not going to be able to see him again, she'll experience all the feelings of loss associated with losing a dad. The only positive about Shaun dying before she was born, and not when she was a toddler or something, was that she'd never had to miss him.

I can't face doing that yet, so until I think of the best way to do it, I'm just putting her off (or to put it more accurately, lying to her) when she asks why he hasn't been round for the last week.

And while I know it's my own fault for chasing after him and bringing this upon myself, 'Just deal with how I'm feeling' is easier said than done. He didn't come over every night, but in the last couple of months it's never been fewer than three days a week. I was starting to get used to having someone next to me in bed again, to the point where it felt strange on the nights I was alone... something I'll just have to get used to again, I suppose.

"Anyway love, can you get a few favourite toys together for me? It's time to go. You'll have a lovely time at Nanny and Grandad's, and tomorrow... you'll be in Year One! I can't believe you're such a big girl."

I've got to go back to Uxbridge, but only for two days this time. Still, they're two pretty big days, or at least one of them is. Jamie starts her second year of school (called Year One, confusingly enough) and I won't be around for it. Still, I suppose it's not as big a deal as her very first day, and I was there for that. And of course, I've told her I want to hear all about her new teacher and the things she's doing when we Facetime in the evenings.

It's just a shame that'll be the only call I'll have to look forward to all night. Sure, I can call Mum or Laura if I fancy a chat, but it's not the same as someone coming all the way down there to surprise me like last time.

Rob came and surprised *me*. Jamie wasn't involved.

I haven't spoken to him after he walked out on me a couple of weeks ago. I think he made it pretty clear he didn't want to hear from me. Doesn't mean it hasn't been hard not to pick up the phone and call him. I've just missed him so much. It's different from the way I missed Shaun. Then, there was nothing at all I could do about it: Shaun was gone, no longer in existence and, hard as it was, I understood

I'd never be able to see him again. Also, I wasn't alone in my grief – lots of people were missing him, people expected me to feel sad and there were always his parents or the counsellors that I could talk to when I needed help with the healing process. I suppose I'm not alone in missing Rob either, but in a different way: there's the five-year-old girl who's come to love him, whose grief will only add to mine.

I can't just do what he did when he had his heart broken, just pack our bags and run away to the next city, or even try the tactic of deleting his number, never going anywhere he'd be and completely forgetting about him. For a start, I guess I'm going to have to talk to him again at least once if he decides to renew his lease. At least that's not for another few months. And not going to the places he'd be is hardly going to stop me thinking about him.

Also, at some point Jamie'll want to go swimming, and what do I do then? She asked last week, saying she wanted to see Rob if he was too busy to come and play with her, and I had to say I knew he wouldn't be there that day - when in fact, I knew it was more likely he would be.

I just don't know if there's any way past this. Last time we spoke, or rather argued, he seemed convinced that when I looked at him, all I saw was Shaun, and as for me... well, I said some stupid things. I know what happened with his ex will have affected him, but I realise now he was just a genuinely nice bloke who loved me and my daughter. I guess I just thought he was too good to be true.

He is true, though. And I can't let him go. When he came to see me in Uxbridge before Christmas, I told Vicky about it the next day, so obviously she asks if he's likely to pop down again this time.

"No. He never actually said the words, 'We're finished', but he left feeling angry and hasn't called me since. I think that's the end of that, don't you? I wouldn't mind," I lie, looking away in case I get upset again, but I manage to get a grip, "but my little girl really liked him. First time I've ever let someone meet her, and now it's ended up like this."

I didn't tell her that Rob was the only one since Shaun, not just the only one Jamie's met. Maybe I should have done, but I didn't really want to give every detail of my life away. It was probably bad enough I told her during our conversation today about how he's a

Crostons' tenant.

"Oh God, girl, what are you doing waiting for him to call?" she asks, in her broad Solihull accent. "You can't just leave it and give up without a fight. You ring him. Tell him you love him, your little girl loves him and you want him back. I'd even forget about the rest of this training and get back up the motorway now, duck."

"I'd go this minute if I thought it'd get me anywhere, but how can I get him to understand I want him for *him*? He's got it into his head that I'm only with him because he's got a couple of similarities to Shaun."

"So hang on, let me get this straight," she says. "Your husband was funny, kind and loved kids, even though he didn't have any, and this Rob's the same?"

I nod, and she continues. "So, what are you supposed to do, go after a complete bastard after that, just to be different? Tell him to sort his head out. The things you love about him are generally good qualities that any woman'd want in a partner. Doesn't make you a weirdo for being attracted to two men who are like that."

Then she laughs. "The height thing is a bit weird though, Nikki. I think you have got 'fess up to having a fetish for giants."

I can live with that. She's completely right. I can't give up on him without at least trying to win him back.

And for once, I know I've not only got to fight, I want to. I never really thought of myself as a weak person in the past: when you're bringing up a child on your own, you can't be. I've been forceful in the past when it came to things like confronting the mum of a kid who kept pushing her in nursery, or persisting in getting the doctor to do tests when they said her allergy was just nappy rash... but if faced with any kind of fight that doesn't involve Jamie, I just roll over and avoid any form of confrontation or change.

But I don’t want to do that this time. Since I've been with Rob, I can feel I've changed, and I don't just mean by not always going for a cheese and ham sandwich every time. Being with him has reminded me what it is to be Nikki again, not just Jamie's mum. I've remembered what it is to have fun, not just get through life.

Most of all, more than any of those things, the biggest way I've changed is that, while we've been separated from each other, I've realised I need him.

After five years of doing everything myself, I'd got used to being alone. If I was writing a set of details on myself, I'd say I was a self-contained, detached, exclusive residence with no permission for extension.

I'm not that person anymore, though. I always equated being alone with being strong, and I could never afford to be anything other than strong as a mum, but maybe I don't have to be two parents for Jamie for the rest of her life. If there's any way I can make him see I love him and not just the idea of trying to replace what I lost in Shaun, then I've got to fight for Rob Jones.

"You're right, Vicky. I'm going to call him now and insist we sort this out."

It goes to his voicemail. Damn, I'm alright with voicemail when I have to leave messages asking whether someone liked the house or whatever at work, but for anything personal, I go to bits.

I hang up. I'd rather not leave a message than some garbled one in which I'll sound like an idiot. Anyway, even if I did leave a message telling him we need to move past this and get back together, I'd only be sitting in my hotel room all night, wondering if he'd read his messages and torturing myself because he hadn't replied.

I'm back on Thursday. I'll speak to him then. If he meant it when he said he loved us, he can't have just forgotten about that in a fortnight. Hopefully it's not too late.

30

I know Vicky was urging me to do a big, rom-com style dash up the motorway before shouting my undying love from the pavement outside Rob's flat like 'Romeo and Juliet' in reverse, but this is real life.

I arrive home at about half-two. Christine knows when I'm due back and has told the school that I'm going to collect Jamie at 3.15 today. The irony is, on an ordinary working day I'd still be in the office and she'd collect Jamie from after-school club at 5, but she's assuming I'd want to do it after being away for a couple of days... and I do, don't get me wrong, but it just means I've got to wait even longer to be able to see Rob and try to sort this out.

When I get to the school, her new teacher (this one looks about 14, she must be Senior Management) tells me how Jamie's been settling in while she gets her coat and reading bag. I'm glad to hear she's settling in alright, except for one thing the teacher says.

"I'm new to this school, Mrs Dunne, so I don't know. Jamie wrote in her journal that she's sad that someone called Rob isn't here anymore. We haven't got a Robert in the year group this year, so was he a friend who moved to another school?"

Well, I think, at least I know her teacher from last year doesn't gossip in the staffroom, before saying, "Erm, I'll speak to her about it. Rob's a... friend. From outside school, actually. I'm trying to make sure she doesn't lose touch with him, but you know what it's like, eh?"

As we leave the school and get into the car, I ask Jamie how her day's been. After the questions about what she had for lunch and if she likes her teacher, I throw in a more contentious one.

"Yes, Mummy. I wish Rob still came to play with me. I wanted him to be my daddy, like Ava-Grace got a new one. I thought he could be mine."

That's it. If I thought I was ready to fight for this before, there's nothing in the world that will stop me now. It might not work: he might not want a relationship with me anymore, and by default have to give up his relationship with Jamie (I can't believe she'd be the cause of him wanting to end things), but I have to know. We have to know.

"Buckle up, Jay. We're going on a ride."

When I pull up outside the leisure centre, Jamie gets excited. "Swimming! Are we going to see Rob?"

"No love, we're not swimming. Look, I need you to be very, very good for me. I just need to talk to someone."

It occurs to me that it's not really ideal to have Jamie with me while I try to talk to Rob. He could accuse me of pulling a low move and using her as emotional blackmail. It's not that at all: I just didn't want to wait 'til tomorrow and I could hardly ask the grandparents to mind her when I've just been away for two days. I can't leave her in the car, so she's just going to have to come with me.

Despite the fact that we don't have any sports bags with us, Sharon beeps our leisure passes and lets us through the barrier into the main part of the centre. Now I just have to find him.

He's usually always in work on a Thursday afternoon, don't think his shift pattern was due to change for a few more weeks.

We walk through to the pool area, which is where I'd find him if he was working today, but he's not around. Jamie looks disappointed.

"Never mind, love, maybe we'll find him another day. Come on, let's go home, yeah?"

I don't want to make any promises about him coming back, though. I can't make things worse than they already are.

"So, Nikki. Uxbridge still as charming as ever?"

I'm in Jeanette's office. She's actually made me a cup of tea and suggested we have five minutes to catch up before we officially open at nine.

Whenever I have to go to Head Office or do training sessions in other branches, Jen and Karen usually just take messages and I deal with them when I return, but if something happens that can't wait, Jeanette handles it.

"Not much to report, really," she says. "Lots of inquiries about the dock apartments, you've got a few viewings booked in for the weekend."

She hands me my mug, and from the way she's acting, I can tell there's a bit more than what she's just told me. At least, knowing Jeanette, she won't hang around too long before getting to the point.

"There was one other thing. Your Rob came in," she says.

I pretend to look for a pen in my bag because I suddenly feel uncomfortable.

"He's not my Rob anymore."

"Well, yes, I sort of gathered that," she continues carefully. "I went and put my foot in it, saying it was odd that he went to the trouble of coming in to the office when he could have just asked you to deal with it directly. He told me he wasn't seeing you anymore. Shame things didn't work out, he seemed really nice."

I sigh. He obviously feels as awkward about this as I do. He'd have known I wouldn't have been around yesterday, I know I'd told him I had another trip to Uxbridge coming up when I booked the hotel. I was kind of hoping he might be interested in coming down with me again, but he couldn't get the time off.

So, he's waited for a day when he wouldn't have to be faced with me, but if he needs some repairs to his flat or whatever, it still falls to me to sort it out – which is going to mean getting back in contact with him, whether I want to or not.

Still, this is my job. Whatever it is, I'm going to have to speak to him and deal with it.

"I can be professional about this, Jeanette, honestly. Just tell me what needs doing."

"Don't worry, I've sorted it," she says. "He came in to ask if there was any way he could end his lease early, at the end of this month instead of January. Usually I'd say it wasn't possible, but when I realised you two weren't together anymore, I thought it might be best to avoid any awkwardness for you. The owner's agreed to it as I've basically promised the flat will either be rented out to someone else immediately, or just this once, Crostons will cover the rent until the lease would have run out anyway."

Right. This is one of those 'careful what you wish for' situations. I wouldn't have liked having to speak to Rob again regarding his flat, and now I don't have to. No, now I'll never have any reason to speak to him again... and I won't know where he is apart from the swimming pool, and that's if he doesn't leave the area completely. That seems to be his preferred way of dealing with things.

Also, I'm amazed by what Jeanette's been prepared to do to help me. She's always been a decent boss, but this is huge. How's she going to explain it if the company has to pay rent on a flat until January, just because I was stupid enough to have a relationship with its tenant?

"Don't worry about that, Nikki. Firstly, I don't think we'll need to. I'm sure someone will take that flat as soon as it becomes empty, but if they don't, I'll arrange something under the Landlord Rent Guarantee insurance. Pretend Rob didn't pay the rent or something. That's not my biggest concern about all this. I'm more worried about you. I wish you'd told me things weren't going well between you and Rob, I had no idea. To be honest with you, I thought the only reason he'd be leaving that flat was if he moved into your house. In fact, that's what I said to him when he asked to end his lease."

That tips me over the edge. The tears I've been trying to hold back escape and run down my cheeks.

"Ha, so did I," I whimper. "I never thought I'd

find anyone I could love the way I loved Shaun, then I met Rob and I really thought he was the one, and I've blown it big time."

Jeanette looks in her drawer, finds a box of tissues and passes them to me.

"Right, stay here. I'll get Jen and Karen to hold our calls, and I'll make us another drink. You can't work while you're like this."

Over another cup of tea, I tell Jeanette everything: how I did notice Rob was a bit like Shaun but didn't see it as a huge issue, but it seems to be one for him, how brilliant he was with Jamie, what I found out about Kayleigh and the row we had the day I got drunk with Laura. Most of all, I tell her how stupid I feel for letting a man who loved me and my little girl go, just because of something that happened in the past.

"You have to talk to him. If he's giving up his flat, maybe he is thinking of leaving the area, and if he does that you really will lose him forever - but he hasn't gone yet. He's still got the keys to the flat for two more weeks. Even if he's moved out early and gone to those friends of his you mentioned,"

"I doubt he could, the whole reason he had to move out in the first place was they needed the space for the baby," I say hopefully.

"You're right, he shouldn't have gone just yet. He'd have to return the keys."

"In that case, why are you still here? Go and find him!" she says, animatedly.

It's only quarter past ten, so my face probably looks a little bemused.

"Go now, that's an order! No point waiting 'til lunchtime, and anyway, you'll be no good moping round the office here if you don't get it sorted. If he's still at the leisure centre, jump into the pool, thrash your arms around a bit and demand to be rescued if you have to, just get him back!"

I stand up and give her a hug. I really don't think any other boss would have been as brilliant about this as she has.

"Thanks, Jeanette. You're amazing. Right, I'll get up there and hope he's still around. Just hope I can call you with some good news later."

"Well, you've never let me down before, Nicola. Don't do it now."

31

"Well, I don't really want to go swimming now, could I just see him? Please?"

When I got to the leisure centre and spotted Rob's car in its usual place, I felt a huge wave of relief to know he was still here. Getting to see him might prove to be a bit harder than I thought, though. I wish Sharon was on reception today. As it is, there's this new bloke who doesn't know me and seems intent on not letting me in because the pool isn't open again until midday.

In the end, possibly to make me go away and stop pestering him if nothing else, he puts an announcement over the Tannoy asking for, 'Rob Jones to the reception area, customer waiting.'

After about five minutes, he comes through the 'Staff Only' door, says, "Alright Pete, who is it?" to the receptionist, who gestures towards where I'm standing.

He looks across at me and his face freezes.

"Nikki," he says eventually. "What are you doing here?"

Despite going through several different versions of what I'd planned to say in my head - both last night and in the car on the drive over here - now it's time to speak, I've got nothing.

"Pete, is the manager's office empty? I think I need to... deal with this in there."

Pete just shrugs, so Rob knocks tentatively on the door at the side of the reception. When he hears nothing, he ushers me inside.

It doesn't look like the sort of office that the general public are usually supposed to come into, so there's only one chair, which he suggests I sit on. I do, but I don't feel any more comfortable.

"I'm not sure this is a good idea, Nikki," he says, avoiding my eyes. "What do you want? Last time I saw you, I didn't think there was a lot more for us to say to each other."

I stand up, but he takes a step away from me.

"Oh come on, Rob, you can't really think that, can you? Are you really willing to pour the last year down the drain because of this one thing? I don't know what I have to say to make you understand I love you for you, not because of Shaun. Okay, I'll admit that I must have a bit of a type physically, but I'm hardly the first person to do that! And as for your personality, yes okay, you are like him in some ways. He was funny, sweet, loving - and you are too. But it's like what Vicky from Solihull said..."

"What, you've been talking about this to someone halfway across the bloody country?"

"She's one of the other Lettings managers, I see her when I'm in Uxbridge. She knows about you because she thought it was really romantic when you came to see me. She told me not to let you go, and said, well she said it's not a crime to want all the things you are just because the last person I loved was like that as well. Then Jeanette said pretty much exactly the same thing. She's even let me come out of work to find you after you saw her about giving up the flat."

When I say that, he turns round to face me from where he's been looking out of the window.

"Right, well, now we've heard the opinions of the estate agency Mafia and they all think I'm making a fuss over nothing. Even if I am, there's the other little thing of you not believing I loved you and I was just trying to get close to Jamie," he says angrily. "Yes, I was hurt by what happened with Kayleigh. I did want to be a dad, but that doesn't mean I was hovering round the pool like some weirdo, preying on single mums so I could hang round with their kids. I really fell for your Jamie, I was ready to see her as my little girl if that was what she wanted - but I loved you first. I can't believe you could think that about me, Nikki."

"Loved?" I ask him. "Is that it, then? I came here to see if there was any chance of us being able to sort things out, but have I just been wasting my time?"

He lets out a sigh of exasperation.

"You know I didn't just forget about you, either of you. I've wanted to call you loads of times over the last couple of weeks. I just didn't know what to say, or whether I'm really what you want."

I move towards him and put my arms out, facing him and touching his elbows.

"Rob, of course you're what I want. I've been so miserable without you. Yes, I had no-one since Shaun, but then I met you and I knew I couldn't be without you. All that stupid business with the earring, the hanging around in that awful pub. I put myself out there again for the first time in years... for you. I thought you were worth it."

He pulls away, opens the door and holds it open, as if he wants me to leave.

"Well you know what, Nikki? You thought wrong. Now, if you don't mind, I have to get back to work. I'll make sure the keys are dropped off to your office before the end of the month."

I don't move. I don't want to leave it like this.

"Rob, can't we...?"

He continues to hold the door, but his tone softens.

"No, I don't think we can." He lets the door close again, before saying, "Believe me, I'm sad about it as well, but maybe some things just aren't meant to be. Hmm, we both knew that before we even met each other, didn't we?" he adds drily.

I pick my bag up from the desk and walk

towards the door but, before I go, I have to ask him something.

"Oh, I'm staying around here, I like this job. I just didn't think it was a great idea that I kept renting that flat."

My lip wobbles a little, but I manage to keep my composure as I think about how I'd had the same thought. Just not for the same reason.

"Fine. Right, well, the way you said the keys would be handed in, not that *you'd* hand them in, I'm guessing Chris or someone'll return them. Just make sure it's by the 30th, please. I'll..."

God, this is hard.

"I'll take Jamie swimming at the other pool across town. You don't have to worry about seeing us again. Bye, Rob."

"Right, well, I guess I'd better... goodbye, Nikki. Tell Jamie..."

It's his turn to hesitate now.

"Tell her... I'm really sorry, but I just couldn't be her dad."

With that, I push the turnstile and leave the leisure centre.

I don't make it to my car without going to pieces, and I don't care. I stop walking, sit on the low brick wall that contains some bushes outside the building and give in to the tears. I think I might have to ask Jeanette if I can just go home; she's been so good about everything else, hopefully she'll understand.

"You all right there, love? What's the matter?"

I look up to see a man in his fifties, wearing shorts and carrying a tennis racquet.

"It's nothing. I'm fine, honestly. I just need to get out of here," I stammer, getting up from the wall and almost breaking into a run to get to my car as quickly as I can.

Once I've locked the door, even though I don't have tinted windows or anything that can hide my face, I feel as though I'm removed from the outside world, so I allow myself to cry once again. I might want to get out of here immediately, but I'm not going to be in any fit state to drive until I've calmed down a bit.

After a few minutes, I feel able to drive away without worrying about having my tears mess up my vision while I drive, so I start the engine. Before reversing out of my space, I look across at the leisure centre for what I guess is going to be the last time. I very much doubt Rob'd be able to bar Jamie and I, but it'd only be awkward and I certainly don't want to subject her to seeing him again.

There's a large window on the first floor, which is next to the entrance to the changing rooms. You'd never usually see a lifeguard stationed there, but Rob's standing in the window, looking straight at my car. Has he been there the whole time, while that man asked me why I was crying and while I've been sitting here?

It doesn't matter, I decide. Either way, he knows why I'm crying - and he doesn't seem to care.

As soon as I've left the car park, I pull over, root around in my bag on the passenger seat and dig out my phone.

"Jeanette? Yeah. No, to be honest I'd say it went the complete opposite. Would you mind if I just didn't come back today? I'll take it as holiday."

After she's told me to go home, sob it out and she'll see me tomorrow, I drive off again, but I don't go home. I need Laura.

32

"Right Nik, no arguments. I'll pick Jamie up from her nan's and give her dinner. You get that down you," she says, handing me a glass of wine that's so big, she's put it one of her juice tumblers.

It's still only 11.45. I'd never normally drink this early in the day, but then I don't get my heart broken every day either. I take a large gulp, which makes me shudder at first, but then the comforting burn seeps into my bloodstream and makes me feel a tiny bit calmer. After a few more sips, I'm feeling numbed enough to talk without my voice jumping the way it does when you're unable to stop crying.

I'm not surprised the alcohol's working so

quickly. I couldn't face any breakfast this morning because I'd been so nervous. Even before what Jeanette told me, I'd been planning to try to approach Rob to try to sort things out. I'd just thought I'd be doing it after I'd had the whole working day to decide what I was going to say, and of course I didn't realise he was taking steps to make sure I wouldn't know where he lived in future.

"So that's it," I moan. "He's made it as clear as he can that he doesn't want anything to do with me anymore. He doesn't want to even talk to me regarding the flat, and he doesn't want me knowing his address. When I said I'd avoid the swimming pool, he didn't tell me not to. I might as well delete him and be done."

My phone's on her kitchen counter, so I pick it up, find 'Robxx' in my contacts and, after hovering for a second, hit 'Delete'.

"Are you sure you should have done that?" she asks, as she tips a tube of Pringles into a bowl.

"Doesn't really matter," I snort. "His number's on the system at work anyway... for a few more weeks. At least this way I won't be able to call him later if I'm drunk."

Anyway, over the next couple of hours, Laura demonstrates why she's the best mate a girl could have. We demolish the Pringles, she gives me another wine (before I insist on a coffee because I don't want to be hammered when Jamie comes home) and pretty much every other sentence she comes out with involves telling me Rob must be mad and how he'll regret what he's done. I can't say she completely succeeds in making me forget about what's happened, but at least I'm not blubbing like a baby anymore.

By five o'clock, the time I'd normally leave work to collect Jamie from my in-laws, I'm sobering up but I still wouldn't be okay to drive, so Laura offers to drive me back to my home, stick around 'til Jamie goes to bed and then get a cab back.

Laura promised not to tell Alan and Christine the real reason why I'd been drinking in the afternoon. I just wasn't sure what they'd think, so we cooked up some story about a corporate client who insisted on plying me with drink at an important lunch and wouldn't take no for an answer.

We get a takeaway (I know I'm going to need to seriously cut back on the junk food if I can't go swimming so often anymore, but not tonight) and take our minds off the day by watching crappy TV 'til Jamie's bedtime, after which Laura calls a cab.

"Just call me if you need anything, okay?" she says as I see her to the door. "What else are best mates for?"

"You've done more than enough already. I don't know what I'd have done without you today, Laura," I say, trying not to yawn because it's definitely been a long day. "I've just got to remember, I've been through worse; I can get through this."

"Yeah, definitely," she says, giving me a last hug. "Talk to you tomorrow. Bye."

After waving her off, I shut the door and sit down.

I guess this is my life from now on: evenings spent alone, watching TV while my daughter sleeps. No conversation, no human contact, no-one next to me when I go to bed. It's the life I had before, and I never complained... but Rob changed things. He changed me. He made me realise there was more to life than what I had – and he made me want to reach out and take it.

I'm not the person I was before I met him; it's hardly surprising that the life I had then isn't what I want anymore.

What about him, though? It looked like he made his feelings pretty clear today: you can't get much more extreme than moving house to avoid talking to someone... I guess I'm just going to have to forget about him. It won't be easy, but I don't have any choice.

I wake up the next day feeling a bit groggy, but not hungover, which is a good job because it's the one of the two Saturdays a month I have to work. At least I had the sense not to start drinking again in the evening. My eyes are a bit red, but a shower and a bit more foundation than usual should sort me out.

While Jamie's eating her cereal, I see that my phone's flashing. I must have forgotten to switch it off before I slunk off to bed early last night.

There's three texts, all from 'Caller Unknown'. Probably just selling something, I think, before noticing that the messages were all sent within a fifteen minute period at around ten o'clock last night.

I open the first one. It's a photo of Bob. That rubber thing Rob kept in his living room. The message consists of a photo of him with a cardboard frown taped to his mouth.

'I'm Bob,' the message says, 'but maybe I should be called Rob...'

What on earth is Rob up to? Only one way to find out, I suppose. Let's look at the second one, which is another picture of Bob, with the cardboard frown and a tear taped to his cheek.

'Because I haven't acted like much of a man. In fact, I've been a total dummy...'

Okay, this sounds like he's feeling a bit bad about what's happened. What's the last message going to say? I click it open, to find a final photo of Bob, this time with a slightly smiling mouth taped on, and an inflatable ring Jamie left behind at his flat round his neck.

'I'd love it if you'd give me a ring? Please, Rob xx'.

I have to sit down. He's had a change of heart! That's got to be what this means.

I'm so excited I can't think straight, but I can't act anything but normally in front of Jamie. Can't go getting her hopes up, she's been disappointed enough already.

Even when I've dropped her off with my mum, I can't just skip round to his flat to see him, eithcr. He's probably got work and I certainly can’t expect to be allowed time off to sort my love life out two days running. I send him a quick text, though: 'Got to work, but yes! Let's talk tonight. N xx'

When I arrive at work, Jeanette invites me into her office and asks how I'm feeling after the previous day's events. She's a little surprised to see me looking so happy. When I've shown her the messages, once again she says she'd be willing to let me go and find Rob to sort things out, but I decline her offer. Now I know he wants to speak to me, and it certainly sounds like he wants to patch things up, I don't mind waiting until after work.

"Well, if you're sure, Nikki," she says. "I'm just glad to see you smiling again. Right, I've got a confession to make. When I told you I'd dealt with the paperwork on Rob's flat," she says, giving me a slightly sheepish smile, "if I'm completely honest with you, I didn't completely cancel his lease... in fact, I didn't do anything with his file at all. I thought if I told you he was planning to leave, you'd be able to change his mind, and well, it does seem to have paid off, doesn't it?"

I'm amazed, but I guess I'm going to have to

tell her I was kind of hoping Rob'd be moving in with me by the end of today. Jeanette, however, seems to know me better than I do myself.

"Still, looks like we're going to have to put my fictional contingency plan into operation anyway, aren't we? By the time you two have kissed and made up tonight, I think you'll be looking for a replacement tenant for Whittaker Street anyway. Am I right?"

She chuckles to herself.

"Oh Nikki, I'm just glad it looks like things are going to work out for you, and not just 'cause you work better when you're not miserable," she tells me as I'm about to leave. "Seriously, I don't think anyone deserves to be happy more than you."

I return to my office and get on with my work for a couple of hours. I expected to be all fluttery and unable to concentrate, but actually, I'm fine. Now that I feel confident that Rob not only wants to talk to me, but the tone of those texts suggests he wants us to try again, I'm able to stop worrying about it and get on with my work.

"Hello. I'm looking for the world's best rental

manager... with the world's stupidest boyfriend."

Rob's standing in the doorway, holding Jamie's inflatable ring that was draped round Bob's neck last night, which he drops when I look up.

I tell the person on the other end of the phone that I'll need to call them back, get up and stand right in front of him. We were standing in the same proximity only about 24 hours ago, but this feels completely different. I look up at him.

"So, those messages. Are we...?"

It doesn't matter that I don't finish the question. He leans in, pulls me slightly off my feet (which I actually didn't like the one other time he did it, but I'm not complaining now) and we kiss. The kind of kiss that makes you realise you don't want to be kissed by anyone else ever again.

"I'm sorry for yesterday, and everything else, Nikki. I just... well, I don't know what I was thinking. But watching you leave yesterday, I knew I couldn't let you go. Whatever's gone on, we can move past it - well, that's if you still want to, of course."

I stand on tiptoes and, in my high heels, just

about manage to kiss him back.

"Rob, I've missed you so much. You've been the only person that's made me feel alive again since... look, neither of us are ever going to forget our pasts, but I want it to be about me and you now. And Jamie. I want to ask you something."

He looks a bit stunned.

"Well, that's what I was going to say," he says, picking up Jamie's ring from the doorway. Of course, Karen, Jen and even Jeanette are all hovering outside the door by now, trying to listen in.

What's he picking that ring up for? He's not planning to use it in some kooky proposal, is he? I hope not. It's not about it being a rubber ring rather than a real one, I don't need any more jewellery: I just don't know if it's the right time. Getting back together's one thing, but I'm not sure we need this pressure.

He's coming toward me with the ring. Oh my God, what am I going to say?

"Well, I was hoping you'd let me give this ring back to Jamie, and let me take her swimming, and... basically be her dad and everything, because I love her, and I love her mum."

He looks at me, waiting for my response.

I break into a loud laugh, then throw my arms round him.

"Yes, absolutely yes," I laugh, then we kiss again. At this point, our audience stops pretending to be checking the notice board and gives us a little round of applause.

Spotting Jeanette, Rob suddenly looks a bit nervous.

"Oh, erm, I'm sorry to be awkward, but it looks like I'm not going to need to leave my flat now after all," he says. "If you haven't told the owner I'm leaving, is there any chance we could just forget about it and I'll stay?"

Jeanette doesn't reply. Instead, she looks across in my direction because she might know what I'm planning but really, this has to come from me.

I take a deep breath. I'm fully aware that I've changed since meeting Rob: I've found determination, spirit, an ability to stand up for myself that I never thought I had. What I'm about to say next, however, might just be the biggest thing I've ever done.

"Well, you know you said you want to be a dad to Jamie?" I begin, taking another breath before coming out with, "Well, a lot of dads live with their little girls... and the mum."

He looks excited, but also a bit concerned.

"But... my lease doesn't end 'til January. What about..."

"There's ways round that, don't worry. Come on Rob, what do you think? I've got three bedrooms, so Bob can have one of his own and we can make sure Jamie doesn't bully him too much," I say, suddenly aware that, if he does turn me down, I've just made a complete fool of myself in front of all my colleagues."

He smiles, looking at me, then over at Jeanette, before turning his attention back to me.

"Well if you're sure, then yeah, let's do this!"

We hug excitedly again, and Karen and Jen return to their desks. Jeanette, however, remains in the doorway.

"Thanks, Jeanette," I say, walking over and giving her a hug. I feel her stiffen in my arms; I don't think she does hugs usually. "You've been brilliant. If it wasn't for you letting me go and see Rob yesterday, I'm not sure this would have happened."

"Oh, I think it would," she says, taking a step away from me, presumably so I can't try to hug her again. "Anyway, as you know, I didn't cancel the lease on the flat, but now you'd better start looking for someone to take the tenancy over. And you," she says to Rob, "I guess you've got some packing to do! Come on, back to work. I'm not having Crostons' Lettings department go to pieces because of all this romantic nonsense," she barks, but I know she's pleased for us really.

When it's just me and Rob in the office again, we have one more kiss before he has to leave.

"I'm so glad you called me, Nikki. Seeing you yesterday made me realise I couldn't be without you. I was stupid to push you away because of... well, you know."

"It's okay," I tell him. "I don't think there's a person in the world who hasn't got some pain in their past. It's how we're going to handle the future that matters now. The three of us are going to be fine, I just know it. Anyway, I've got to get back to work now, but why don’t you come round tonight and we'll tell Jamie the good news?"

THE FINAL CHAPTER

I was right. The three of us have been fine. Jamie was over the moon at the thought of having Rob back in her life, even more so at the thought of having him around all the time. It finally felt like everything had fallen into place: she had the dad she'd always felt she missed out on, Rob got a family to be part of, and I... well, I got him. And I found out what it was like to be me again.

Thankfully, when it happened four months after he'd moved in with us, the proposal didn't involve life-rings or any other daft stunts. We were just having a quiet night watching the telly in the second week of January. He said something sweet about how he didn't have post-Christmas blues, because since he'd found me, life couldn't get any better. I remember saying something in agreement and snuggling into him as we sat on the couch together. Then, he said the only thing that could make it better was if he wasn't just Jamie's dad, but my husband as well.

I didn't even have to think about my answer. Sure, I was happy enough as we were, but the thought of us making the relationship permanent, promising to be together for life... that would make everything perfect.

The wedding really was the best day of my life, and despite some of the hard times, there's quite a bit of competition for that accolade these days. Neither one of us wanted a ridiculous fancy affair, but we did have a bit more fuss than my first wedding. If his family were coming over *en masse* from Congleton, we guessed we'd better make it worthwhile.

Chris was Rob's best man and of course, no matter how simple we wanted to keep it, we had to have the one bridesmaid. I remember Jamie spent the whole day beaming and delightedly showing off her dress, 'And high heeled shoes, look!', lifting her hem to reveal pale blue shoes with the tiniest of raised heels.

I didn't want a wedding dance this time either;

I'd have felt far too self-conscious after seeing so many videos on the internet of people who must have gone and had dancing lessons and probably got really stressed out, when I just wanted us to enjoy the day. Instead, Laura did what she does best: after spending the afternoon doing face painting for the younger guests (which got a little, erm, interesting after she'd had a couple of drinks), she picked up a microphone once again and hosted a pub-style quiz, in which all of the questions were based upon me and Rob: how we met, likes and dislikes and whether or not we could remember the other one's shoe size. Fabulous - and once again, I won.

In fact, the only thing that's been at all bad recently is the reason I'm here at the pool now. At the playground a couple of weeks ago, I gave Jamie a rather energetic push on a swing, so my shoulder's started hurting again. Obviously, these days I have my own personal massage service, but Rob's not a qualified physio, so I thought I'd come back to Aqua Therapy. It certainly gave me a result last time.

It's been a while since the original injury, so I don't think Jeanette feels as responsible as she did before. I'm able to come out to do the class at lunchtime once a week, but I'm making up the time by cutting back on breaks on other days. I don't mind, that's fair enough – and anyway, my favourite lifeguard's always on duty on Tuesdays.

Once in the pool, I find a space and twirl around, extending my arms to ensure I'll have enough space around me when we start moving. The instructor, as chirpy and enthusiastic as ever, surveys the pool, full of heads bobbing in the water and says, "Okay everyone, you know what I've got to ask."

I glance across at Rob and he gives away a hint of a smile, but otherwise manages to keep his face straight. I don't say anything. We've only got to keep it quiet for a few more weeks, but when we can tell people, Jamie's got to be first.

ABOUT THE AUTHOR

Sue Bordley lives on the Wirral, Merseyside
with her husband and two children.
She smells a bit of chlorine.